Elementary Drawing Simplified

Elementary Drawing Simplified

PREFACE.

This work is divided into two books.

The first book, "Drawing Simplified," is a regular and complete course in Representative Drawing, adapted to pupils of the upper grades and for self instruction. It is to be placed in the hands of the pupils.

The second book, "Elementary Drawing Simplified," is adapted to the pupils of the lower grades, and for the general instruction of the teachers in those grades. It is not to go into the hands of the pupils, but to guide the teacher. A knowledge of the first book is necessary for successful work in the second.

The same general plan is pursued in each book, and each step is illustrated and carefully graded.

FORM STUDY AND DRAWING.

BOOK II.

PRIMARY DRAWING.

In primary drawing, the teacher must be thoroughly prepared. Thorough preparation is the key to her success. She must know her lesson so well as to be independent of the book. She must be able to place the drawing on the blackboard and assist her pupils from memory. This is easy and simple if the principles of drawing are understood.

The process of preparing a lesson is as follows: (1) The drawing or drawings to be used in the lesson should be carefully drawn on paper. (2) It should be drawn on paper from memory. If copying the drawing once is not sufficient, draw it a second or even a third time, and then draw from memory. (3) Draw on the blackboard from memory. (4) Use it in the class.

The strongest powers possessed by the child to which the teacher of drawing can appeal are (1) perception, (2) memory, (3) imitation, (4) imagination.

When teaching drawing to children, these faculties may be appealed to with the assurance of a ready response. The reasoning powers are not sufficiently developed to be depended on to any great extent, but the child sees, remembers, imitates, and imagines in the superlative degree.

A little girl *sees* her mother make cakes and pies, *remembers* the process, *imagines* mud to be dough, and *imitates* her by making cakes and pies from mud.

A little boy *sees* his father harness the horse, *remembers* the lines and bits, *imitates* him by putting a rope in the mouth of a playmate, and *imagines* him a real horse.

To analyze the object may be of great value to the mature mind, but to the child, it is of little importance as an aid in teaching him how to draw. For example, teach a child all about a cube — that it has six faces, eight corners, twelve edges, etc. — and seemingly he is no nearer to knowing how to draw the cube than he was before. On the other hand, teach the child how to draw the cube by example and do so with little explanation and much work, and in a short time, the child, by means of his strong perceptive and imitative powers, will not only be able to draw the cube but can tell about its faces, corners, and edges as well.

Teach children how to draw as they learn how to swim.

Explain to a child the process of swimming, analyze each movement, tell him how to use his arms and legs, how to strike out, and then send him into the water. He will drown. He cannot swim a stroke. But if you take the child into the water with you and let him *see* you swim, he will learn how, even without a word of explanation. Children learn best by seeing and doing.

Children will not learn how to draw by you telling them how, any more than the boy will learn how to swim by the same process.

The child must see you draw. You must lead the way. They must see before they imitate.

Place the child in his seat with a tablet of paper and a pencil at his service, and you step to the blackboard and draw a picture of interest to the child. He will draw, and he will learn, even without a word of explanation.

Children learn how to draw by drawing, more rapidly than by all other means combined. Therefore, let the watchword be, "To learn how to draw, you must draw." Let this be the central idea in every recitation, and let no day pass without putting it in force.

THE SPHERE.

Secure attention[1].

Children are less embarrassed when doing than when talking. Give them something to do at once. Teach the right hand and the left hand.

The class may stand. "James, which is your right hand? You may hold up your right hand. You may hold up your left hand. All may hold up the right hand. All may hold up the left hand. All may put the right hand on top of the head. All may put the left hand on top of the head. Susie, where is your left hand? Hold your right hand out. All may hold the right hand out. All may hold the left hand out."

Teach the right and left side, the right and left foot, in the same manner.

1   It is not the design in this department to give arbitary rules to guide teachers. We take it for granted that each teacher has methods and devices of her own, which, in her hands are quite as effective as any that can be given. We would have every teacher feel free to work independently. The aim here is to give plenty of material to work with, and general suggestions how to use it.

After sufficient drill of this kind to put the class at ease, take a sphere in your hand and lead the class by means of questions to tell you what it is. Get them interested in the sphere.

Hold the sphere in one hand and, with the other, draw an outline of it on the blackboard similar to Fig. 1.

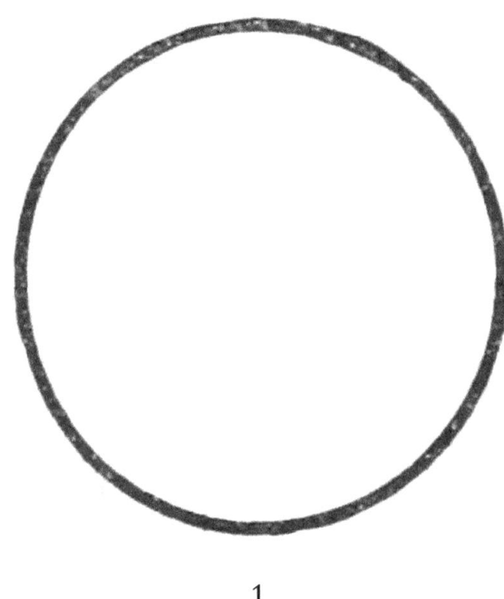

1

The pupils see the sphere. They know what it is. They see you draw the outline on the blackboard. They recognize the resemblance. They see the relation between the sphere and the drawing on the blackboard. They see. Let them imitate by drawing the sphere on their tablets, from the outline on the blackboard.

Look at their drawings frequently and have a kind word for each earnest effort. Be patient with those who are slow to learn.

If any are holding the pencil in a cramped manner, correct them, but do not insist on holding the pencil in a particular position or after a prescribed rule. No particular way is natural and easy and hence cannot be right. *Give the individuality of the child as much freedom and independence as possible.* The same may be suggested about sitting in the seat. While no particular rule can be given for all, still cramped and unnatural positions should be corrected at once, and the pupils required to sit erect with their feet square on the floor.

Let the class draw the sphere a number of times, as many times as you can keep up their interest in it.

Do not compel them to draw, but lead them to do it by drawing on the blackboard and encouraging them to do likewise.

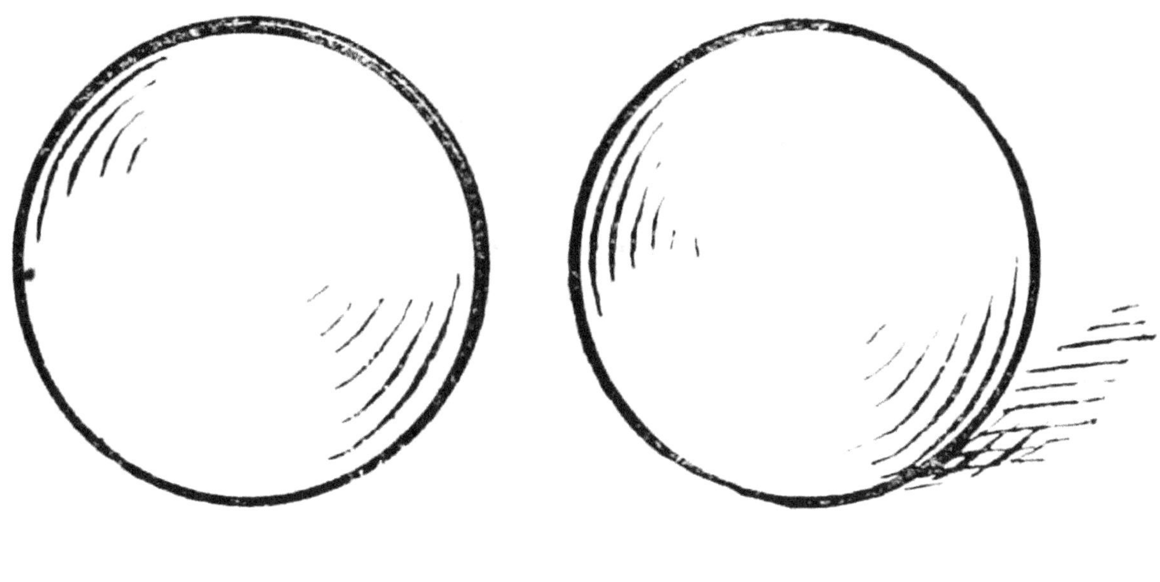

To each sphere that you draw, add some marks of expression as in Figs. 2 and 3. Do not speak of these marks or attempt to explain them[2], but let the child see and use them unconsciously.

Teach the name "*sphere.*"

Draw a large sphere on the blackboard where all can see it, similar to Fig. 4, and leave it until the next lesson.[3]

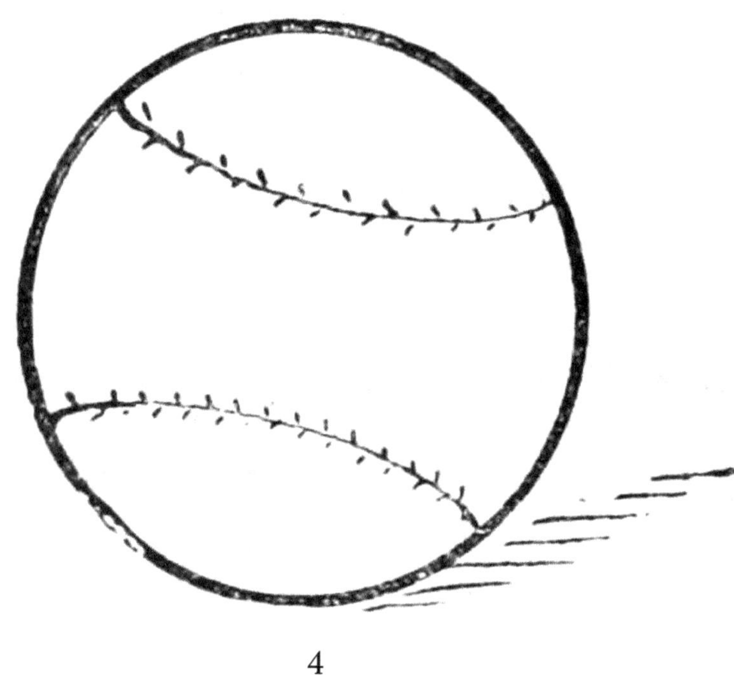

4

What is shaped like a sphere?[4] Ask the pupils to bring objects to school similar to a sphere,

2 There are certain steps in drawing which cannot be easily explained. It is best to say nothing about them and let the child unconsciously absorb them. Do not attempt to explain lines of expression.

3 Children learn a great deal by unconscious absorption. A drawing left on the black-board similar to the lesson is a silent teacher.

4 The principal common objects shaped similar to a sphere are: croquet, base and foot balls, globe,

thus cultivating the habit of observation. Use the objects brought to school for the lesson.

For example, an apple has been brought to school as an object that resembles a sphere.

Hold the apple in one hand before the class. What form does it resemble? How does it differ from the sphere? etc.

5

Hold the apple in one hand, and with the other, draw it on the blackboard as in Fig. 5. They see the apple and recognize its resemblance to the drawing on the blackboard. They see. Let them imitate by drawing the outline on their tablets.

Teach the right and left side of the drawing. Place a mark on the right side of the drawing.

marble, apple, peach, orange, pumpkin, squash, grape, cherry, plum, gooseberry, currant, etc. There are many others not spherical in form, but still are nearly so, and may be taught in connection with the sphere more easily than by making separate groups. These are: pear, lemon, potato, tomato, onion, egg, turnip, melon, etc.

"Mary, you may tell me which side of the apple the mark is on," etc.

Teach the top side and the bottom side of the apple. "James, you may tell which side of the apple the stem is on," etc.

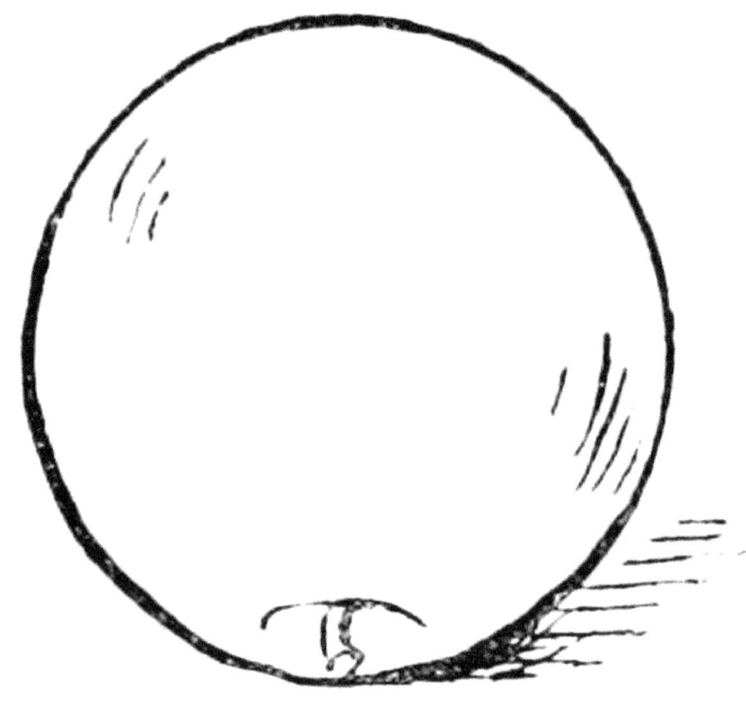

6

Hold the apple in one hand and, with the other, draw the apple with the stem pointing downward, as in Fig. 6. "Sara, you may tell which side of the apple the stem is on."

In like manner, draw an apple with the stem pointing to the right and to the left, as in Figs. 7 and 8, each time letting the class see that you draw from the apple you have in your hand.

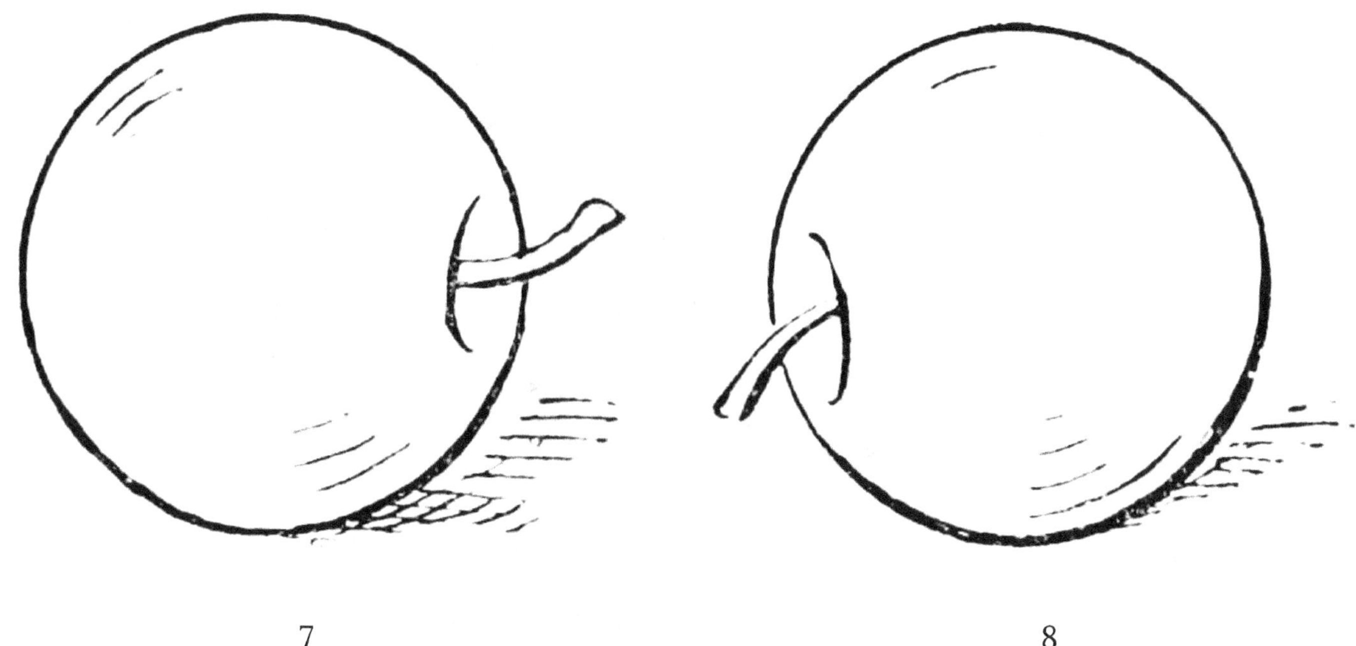

7   8

Let the class copy each drawing you make.

Send the class to the blackboard[5] and, by dictation, drill the pupils on what they have had.[6] Draw a sphere. Draw an apple with the stem on top. Draw an apple with the stem on the bottom. Draw an apple with the stem pointing to the right. Draw an apple with the stem pointing to the left.

5   The black-board should be used often. It is well to let the class (1) Reproduce the lesson of the day before. (2) Draw familiar objects from memory. (3) To hold objects in one hand and draw them with the other.

6   If the pupils are not able to draw the apple from memory let them copy the apple until they are able.

Show two apples of unequal size and draw them on the blackboard similar to Fig. 9.

9

Draw one with the stem up and the other with the stem down, as in Fig. 10.

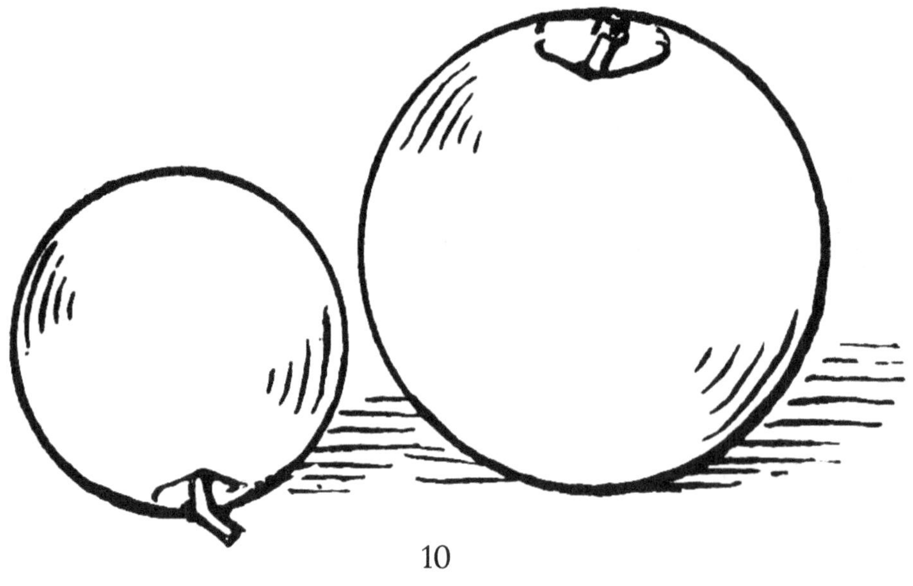

10

Draw Fig. 10 with the stem of one pointing to the right and the stem of the other pointing to the left.

Drill with the class at the blackboard.

Draw a large and a small apple side by side.

Draw a large apple with a small one on its right, with the stem on the bottom.

Draw a small apple with a large one on its right, with the stem pointing to the right, etc., etc.

Place three apples before the class and draw them on the blackboard as in Fig. 11.

11

Place one large apple before the class with a small one on each side. Draw them on the blackboard as in Fig. 12.

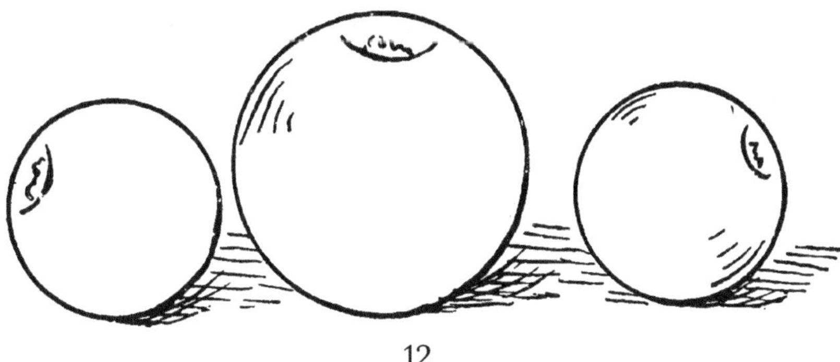

12

Drill at the blackboard.

Procure a round apple, a long apple, and a broad apple similar to those in Fig. 13. Show the apples to the class and ask questions that will lead them to see the difference in form. Place them in a row before the class.

13

Draw each apple separately and let the class copy.

Draw a group composed of a round and a broad apple.

Draw a group composed of a broad and long apple.

Draw a group composed of a long, broad, and round apple.

Draw a long apple with the stem pointing up, down, right, left.

Drill at the blackboard.

Draw a round apple.

Draw a broad apple.

Draw a long apple.

Draw a long and a broad apple.

Draw one broad and two long apples, etc., etc.

Place one apple behind another so that the class can see the whole of one and part of the other, as shown by half of group 14 (A and B). Ask questions: Can you see all of the first apple? Can you see all of the second apple? Why can't you see all of the second apple? Etc., etc.

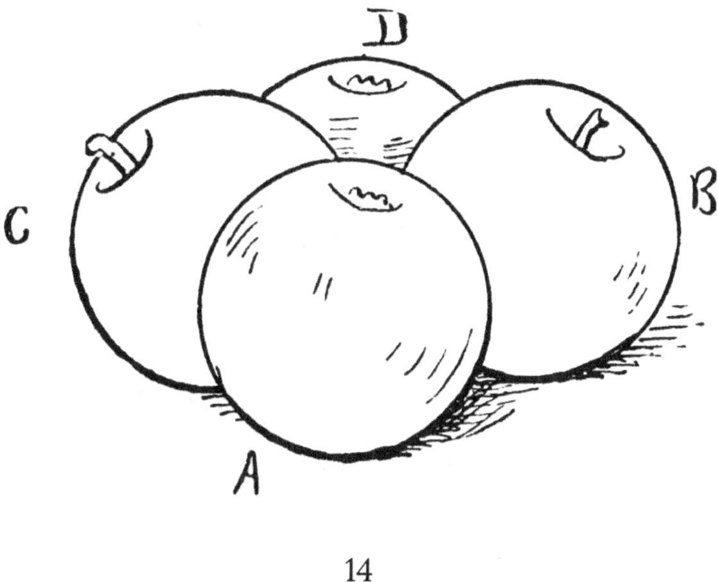

14

Draw apples A and B (Fig. 14) on the blackboard.

Draw apples A and C.

Draw apples A, B, and C.

Draw the whole group, Fig. 14.

Drill at the blackboard.

Draw two apples, one behind the other.

Draw a group of three apples.

Draw a group of four apples.

Place a group of four or five apples before the class, similar to Fig. 15. Ask questions about the group: How many apples in the group? How many can you see? How many can you see the whole of? How many can you see a part of? How many rest on the table? Etc., etc.

15

Draw the group on the blackboard, and let the class copy.

Drill at the blackboard by giving a problem to each one adapted to their ability. Mary, you may draw an apple on the blackboard with the stem sticking from the right side. John, you may draw a large and small apple. Henry, you may draw a long apple, etc., etc.

Show a good apple and a bad apple to the class.

Ask questions of comparison.

A moral story in connection with this lesson would be appropriate.

Draw the good and bad apples on the blackboard, as in Fig. 16. Let the class copy.

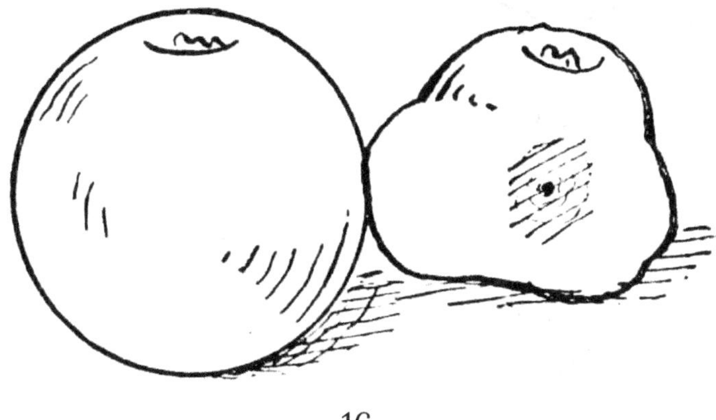

16

Drill at the blackboard.

Let each draw from dictation. John, you may draw a group of three apples. Henry, you may draw a group consisting of a round, a long, and a broad apple. Mary, you may draw a good and bad apple, etc., etc.

Lead the class to draw original groups. This may be done through dictation by gradually making the oral direction less until the whole problem is left with the pupil.

For example: John, you may draw a large apple with a small one on each side. John, you may draw a group of three apples. John, you may draw a group of apples.

The pupils have *seen*, they have *imitated*, they *remember*, and now they *imagine* and begin to *reason*.

Any of the objects represented by Figs. 17 - 34 may be substituted in place of the apple or used with it.

Two or more objects, such as an apple and pear, potato and turnip, melon, squash, and pumpkin, may be grouped together.

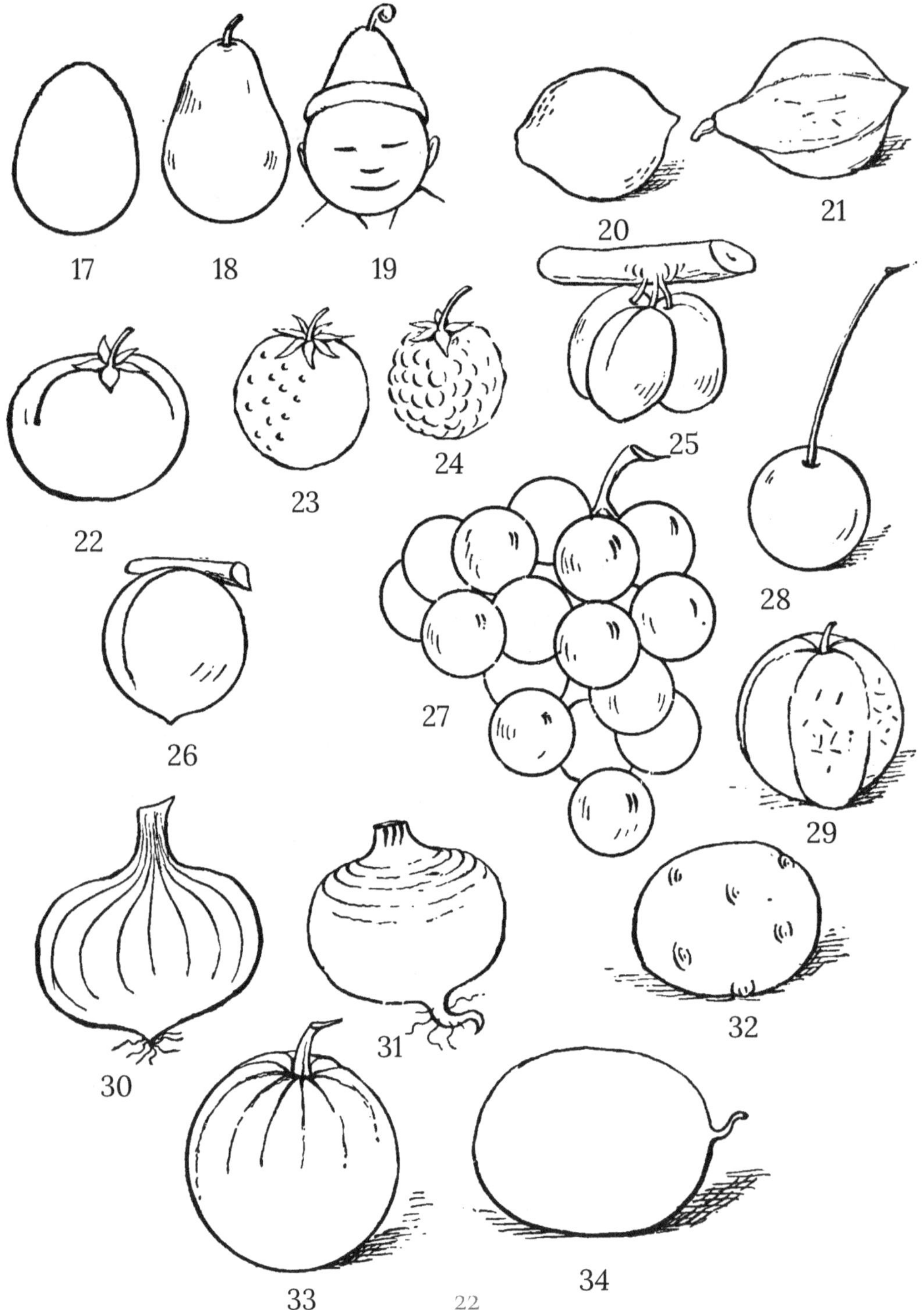

17
18
19
20
21
22
23
24
25
26
27
28
29
30
31
32
33
34

DRAWING FROM THE REAL OBJECT[7].

As soon as you think best, gradually substitute the real object for the drawing on the blackboard. This is not an easy task and requires tact and patience. Do not compel pupils to draw from the real object, but lead them easily and gradually from one to the other.

Three steps are necessary to lead the child to draw from the real object:

1. Let the child see you draw the object. (Perception).

2. Let the child copy the object you have drawn. (Perception and imitation).

3. Let the child draw the real object. (Perception, imitation, and reasoning).

Care must be taken not to hurry the pupil from the second to the third step. It is necessary to lead him gradually at this point, and allow him to copy your drawings on the blackboard many times in different positions before it is advisable for him to draw from the real object.

For example, you have been teaching the child how to draw the apple. He has become familiar with it. He can draw a large apple, a small apple, different-shaped apples, and groups of apples.

7   This is perhaps the most critical point for the pupil in drawing. It is at this point the pupil is most likely to acquire a dislike for the work. Drawing from the real object is to the child difficult, dry and uninteresting as compared with drawing from a picture placed on the black-board by the teacher, and if care is not taken the result is to make the child dislike drawing.

He has seen you draw them from apples you have held in your hand or placed on the table.

Now give the child an apple and let him draw it on the blackboard. If he hesitates or lacks confidence in himself, you take the apple and draw it, and then lead him to do so. Encourage each step. Do not drive. Lead. Be patient.

Care must be taken not to weary the pupils. A class that is not interested learns very little.

Place an apple on the desk before each pupil and let them draw it.   Lead them in the same manner as above.

An object as large as a melon (Fig. 34), a squash (Fig. 21), or a pumpkin (Fig. 33) may be placed before the class where all can draw from the same object.

TEACHING OBSERVATION.

The sphere should be made the key to all similar forms. To do this is a very important duty. To show that the sphere is similar to an apple, a pear, a haystack, and like forms, unifies the powers of observation and the whole work of form study.

Observation should be directed so as:

1. To show the application of the general or type form to special forms.

2. To teach comparison.

3. To teach unity.

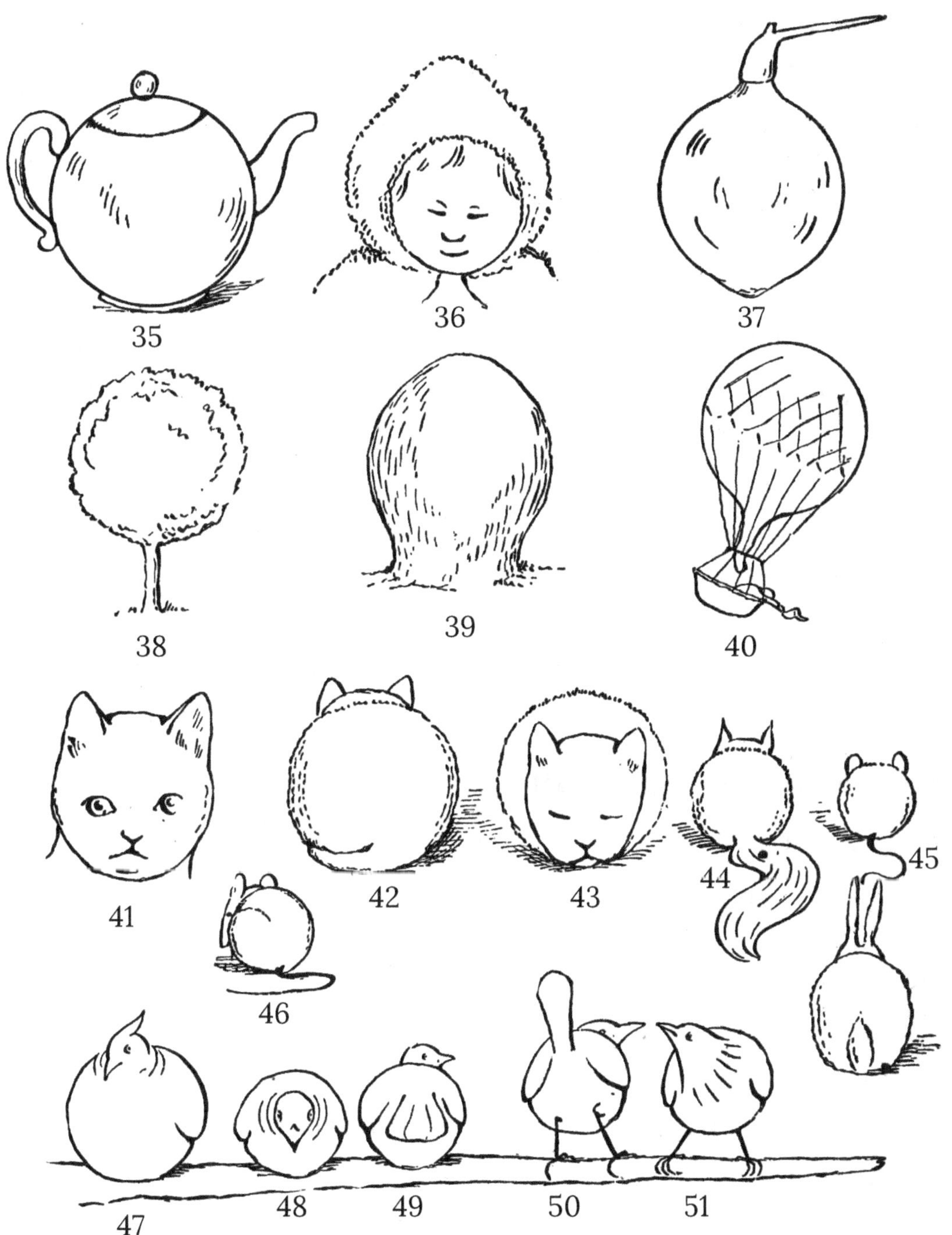

35
36
37
38
39
40
41
42
43
44
45
46
47
48
49
50
51

The application of the type form to special forms may be applied:

(1) To objects that resemble the sphere, such as Figs. 23, 24, 26, 27, 28, and 33. (2) To objects that resemble the sphere in part, as Figs. 17, 18, 20, 21, 30, 31, 34, etc. (3) To objects that seemingly do not resemble the sphere, as Figs. 41–52.

An excellent way to teach observation is to:

1. Lead each pupil to make a list of all the round objects he can find.

2. Draw a sphere on the blackboard and then turn it into Figs. 17 - 52, and lead the pupil to make like comparisons with the real objects.

3. Lead the pupil to make special comparisons.

Draw the egg (Fig. 17) on the blackboard and turn it into a pear (Fig. 18) by adding a stem to it. If possible, show an egg and pear to the class. If this is not convenient, ask each pupil to examine them and notice their similarity of form.

In like manner, draw a lemon and turn it into a squash (Figs. 20 and 21).

Draw an onion and turn it into a turnip (Figs. 30 and 31).

Draw a tomato (Fig. 22), and show that the stem is similar to that of a strawberry (Fig. 23) and a raspberry (Fig. 24) by substituting the body of the strawberry and the raspberry in place of the tomato, using the same stem.

Draw a sphere on the blackboard and turn it into a tree (Fig. 38), and ask the class to see if they can find a similar one on their way home.

Draw a sphere and turn it into a cat's head (Fig. 41), and ask the pupils to notice whether the cat's head is like it.

Draw a sphere and turn it into a cat similar to Figs. 42 or 43, and ask the class to try and see the cat in a similar position.

Draw a sphere and turn it into birds (Figs. 47 - 51), and ask each pupil to try and see birds in similar positions.

These transitions from the type form to special forms are a simple and effective method of teaching unity — the ability to see objects as a whole.

To change a sphere into a cat, a squirrel, a rabbit, or even an apple requires one to see or think of an object as a whole. This is very important in drawing.

53   54   55   56

DEVICES[8].

After children have drawn the same object a number of times, it becomes wearisome to them. In order to keep up the interest necessary to ensure close attention, various devices may be employed. For example, the sphere in itself is not interesting to children, and they soon tire of it, perhaps long before they have mastered all that is required of them. It is at this point the device comes into use.

Though the children may not be interested in the sphere itself, a kitten peeping over the top, as in Fig. 54, changes the conditions entirely, and interest is once more restored.

Figs. 53 - 65 are devices that may be used with the sphere or forms similar to it.

---

8 Care must be taken not to let the device become primary and the object you are teaching secondary. Do not use a device until it is necessary, and then use it sparingly.

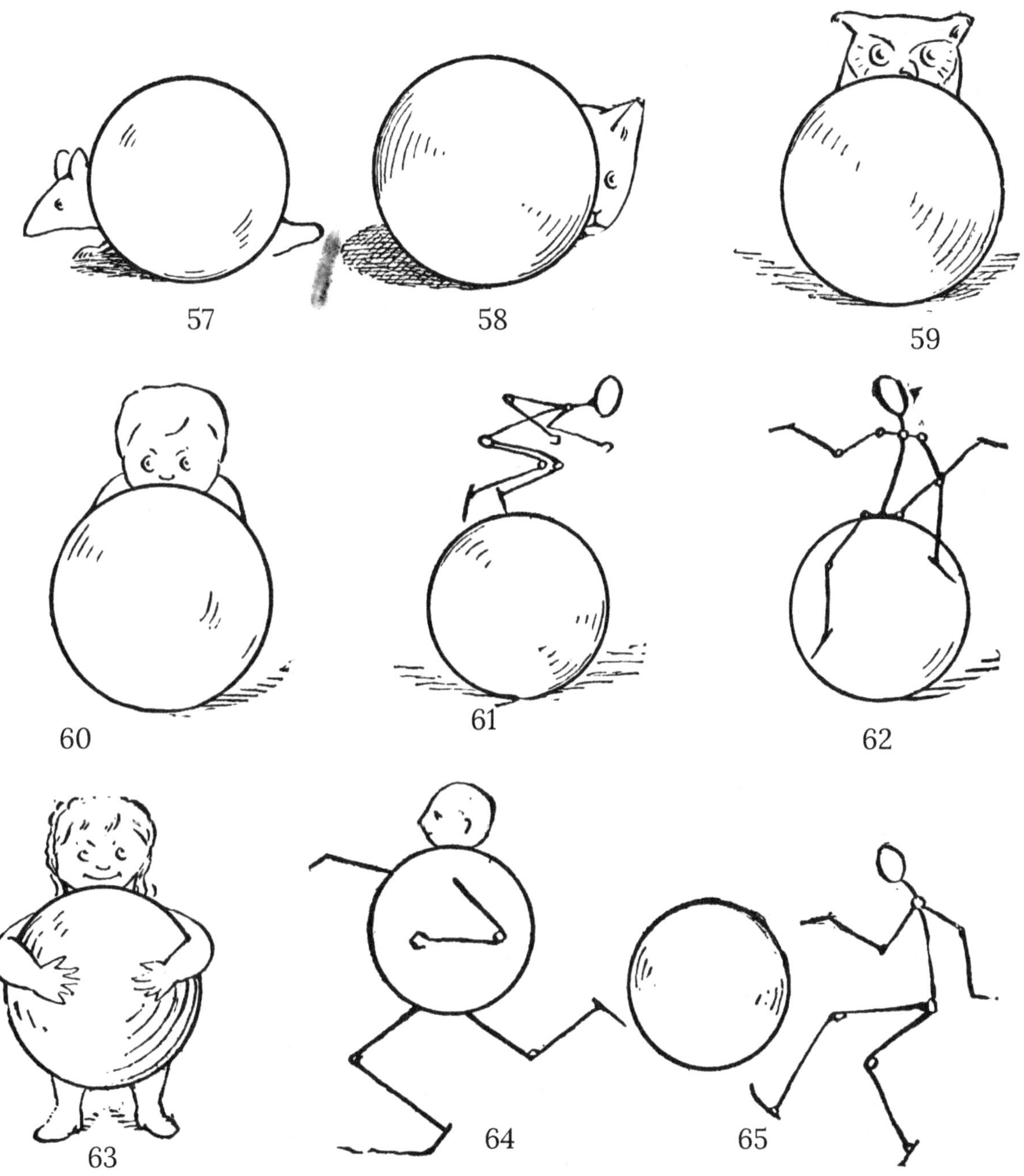

57
58
59
60
61
62
63
64
65

These devices are to awaken an interest in the mind of the child. They are to be used sparingly and only when necessary to gain attention.

Do not let the device become primary and the form you are teaching secondary. Remember, it is the type form that is being taught, not the device.

The device may be drawn as a part of the drawing lesson, but it should not receive much attention.

Devices may be divided into two classes:

1. Devices that may be introduced with the type form before the class, as in Fig. 53.

2. Devices that appeal to the memory or imagination, as in Figs. 54 - 65.

The use of devices in increasing interest is based largely on *curiosity* and *love of surprise*[9], which is strongly developed in children. The curiosity to know what you are going to draw, what you are drawing, and surprise at what you do draw rouses the mind to action and concentrates the energies on the lesson.

Associate that which is agreeable to the child with that which you wish it to draw. For example, if the child is drawing a pear and the work is becoming irksome, there is much gained by enlivening the work by stepping to the blackboard, drawing the pear as in Fig. 18, and changing it into Fig. 19. These changes amuse and instruct at the same time. Often, the greatest truths are taught by the most simple devices.

9   Children love that which is unexpected and surprising. They love to trace familiar among complicated forms. To trace similarity in forms widely different. Children trace all sorts of fancies in the frost work on the window, and see strange forms and shapes in the "big bag of cotton" clouds that rise above the horizon. Use these strong forces in the drawing class.

The hand of the little child is usually able to execute as rapidly as the mind is able to conceive. For this reason, it is not best to give the hand special training, but rather to train the hand and mind together.

The mind is primary, the hand secondary. The proper way to train the hand is through the mind. For example, if you wish to train the hand to draw straight lines, do not give the child straight lines alone to draw, but give them objects that contain straight lines, objects that require as much brain as hand work, and develop both mind and hand together.

Compelling a child to draw straight and curved lines as a special hand exercise will make the child dislike drawing.

It is best to commence and finish a new drawing each day, or perhaps several drawings of the same object. Let rapidity and accuracy go hand in hand. There is no excuse for that slow, laborious drawing that requires lesson after lesson to finish. The primary department is not the place for such work.

PART II.

THE CUBE.

The study of the cube is divided into three parts: (1) When one face of the cube is seen. (2) When two faces of the cube are seen. (3) When three or more faces of the cube are seen.

WHEN ONE FACE OF THE CUBE IS SEEN.

Under this heading and in the order given, teach: (1) Edges. (2) Corners. (3) The vertical line. (4) The horizontal line. (5) The rectangle.

1

FIGURE 1. - (1) Place a common crayon box before the class in such a manner as to show one face as indicated by the illustration, and draw it on the blackboard.

(2) Teach the edges of the box.

(3) Ask the class, pointing to the box, how many edges they can see.

(4) John, you may take the pointer and point to each edge.

(5) Begin at once to connect the drawing on the blackboard and the box.

(6) Lead the class to point to an edge on the box, and then to the corresponding line in the drawing on the board.

(7) Let the class draw a similar box on their tablets.

(8) It is best to speak of "*edge*" as referring to the box and "*line*" as referring to the drawing.

DEVICES.

A simple outline of the face of the box is not interesting to children, but it may be made so by means of devices.

Devices may be divided into two classes: (1) Those that can be introduced with the box before the class, as Figs. 1-12.

(2) Those appealing to the memory or imagination, as Figs. 13-24.

The primary use of devices is to interest the pupil and to stimulate them to greater exertion.

Care must be taken not to allow the device to become primary and the object you are teaching secondary.

Devices should be used sparingly and only when necessary.

Devices should be simple and easy to represent.

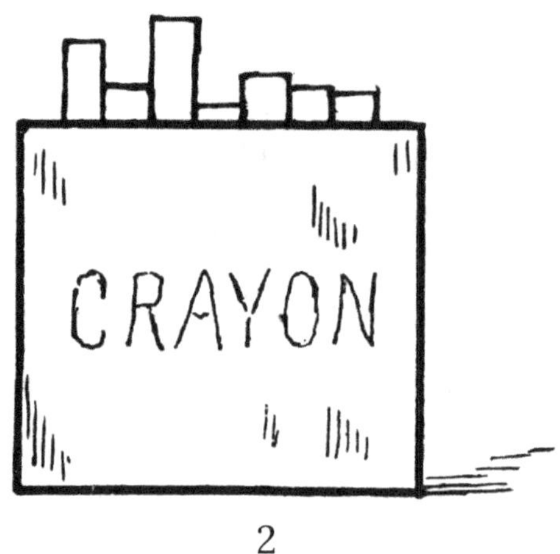

FIGURE 2. – (1) Place the box before the class and then draw it on the blackboard.

(2) Let the class draw a similar one.

(3) Teach the corners.

(4) Mary, you may take the pointer and point to each corner on the box. Point to each corner in the drawing on the board. Point to the upper right-hand corner on the box. Point to the same in the drawing.

(5) James, you may take the pointer and point to the lower right-hand corner of the box, the lower left-hand corner, and the upper left-hand corner. Point to the lower right-hand corner in the drawing, the lower left-hand corner, and the upper left-hand corner.

(6) Pull some of the crayon sticks partway out of the box and secure them by pushing the cover against them.

(7) Represent them in the drawing. Let the class do the same.

(8) Print the word "crayon" on the box.

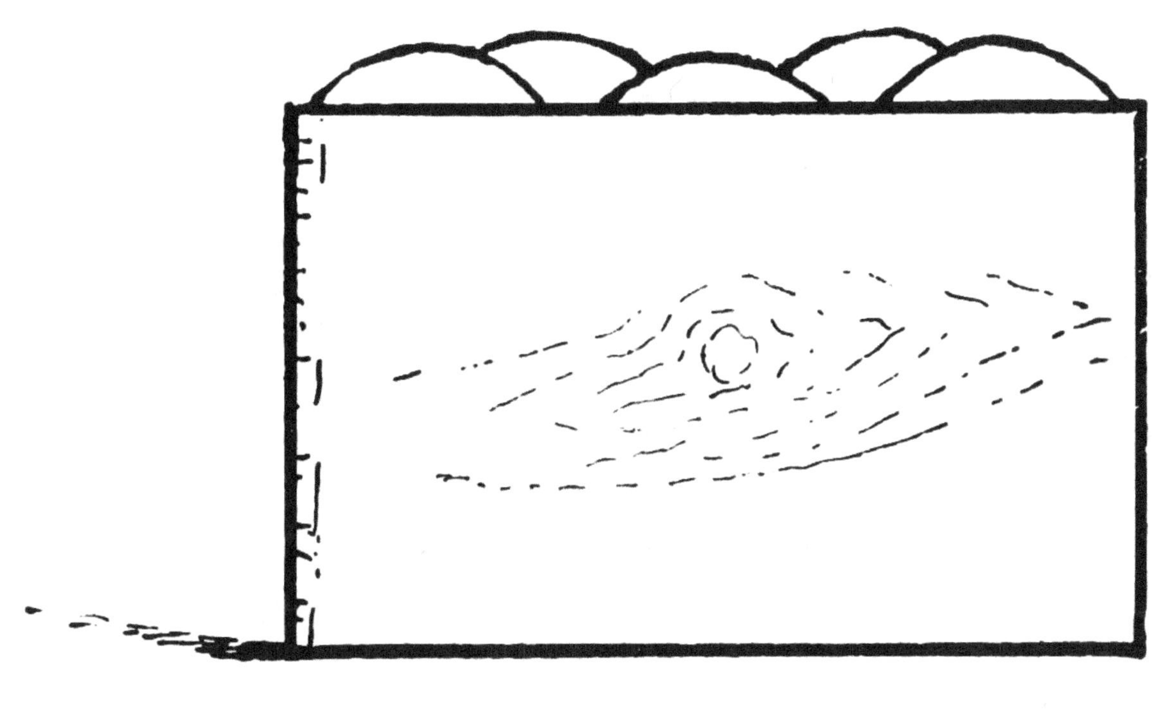

3

FIGURE 3. - (1) Compare the side with the end of the box by asking questions of the class.

(2) Review corners and edges.

(3) Place the box before the class and draw it on the blackboard.

(4) Let the class draw a similar one.

(5) Fill the box with balls, or place one ball in it, so that it will show above the edge.

(6) Represent it in the drawing, and let the class do likewise.

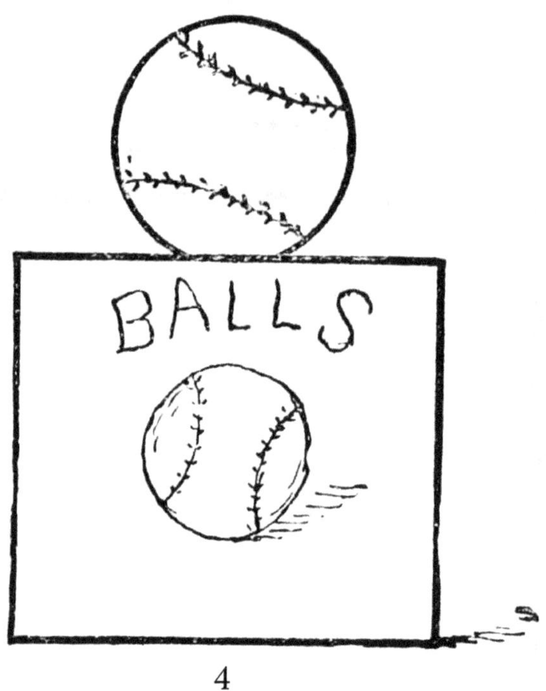

4

FIGURE 4. - (1) Hold the end of the box toward the class.

(2) Susie, you may take the pointer and point to each corner and edge: the top edge, bottom edge, right edge, and left edge.

(3) Draw the box on the blackboard and let the class draw a similar one.

(4) Let a member of the class point to the lines and corners in the drawing and the corresponding edges on the box.

(5) Place a ball on the box, and represent it in the drawing.

(6) Draw the picture of a ball on the box.

(7) Print the name "balls" on the box.

5

FIGURE 5. - (1) Place the box before the class and then draw it on the blackboard.

(2) Let the class draw a similar one.

(3) Fill the box nearly full of paper or some other convenient substance and then place a few cherries so that they will show above the edge. Represent these cherries in the drawing, and let the class do likewise.

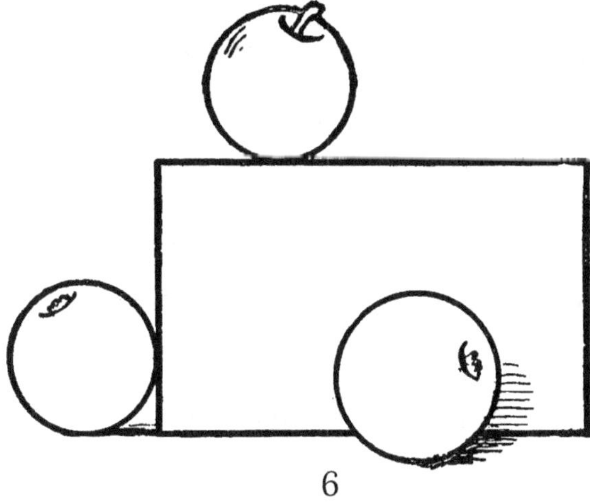

6

FIGURE 6. - (1) Place the box before the class and draw it on the blackboard.

(2) Teach the vertical and horizontal lines.

(3) James, you may take the pointer and point to a vertical edge on the box, a vertical edge in the room. Hold the pointer vertically. Point to a vertical line in the drawing. Draw a vertical line on the blackboard.

(4) Peter, you may take the pointer and point to a horizontal edge on the box, a horizontal edge on your desk, a horizontal edge in the room. Hold the pointer in a horizontal position. Point to a horizontal line in the drawing. Draw a horizontal line on the blackboard.

(5) Place an apple upon the box and represent it in the drawing.

(6) Place an apple by the side of the box and represent it in the drawing.

(7) Place an apple this side of the box and represent it in the drawing.

Cut from cardboard or similar material three sizes of each of the following figures, and keep them together in a box for use in the class: (1) An equilateral triangle. (2) A right-angled triangle. (3) A square. (4) A rectangle. (5) A circle. (6) An ellipse.

A rectangle is spoken of here as being longer than wide to distinguish it from the square.

7

FIGURE 7. - (1) Place the box before the class in such a manner as to show the cover, and draw it on the blackboard.

(2) Teach the rectangle. Hold one side of the box toward the class and lead the pupils to see that this peculiar figure is a rectangle. Show the end of the box and lead them to see that it is similar to the side in shape. In like manner, show the top and bottom of the box.

(3) Draw three rectangles on the blackboard similar to Figs. 1, 3, and 7, and ask questions of comparison.

(4) Trace a rectangle in the air with your finger. Ask the class what figure it is. Trace a long rectangle horizontally. Trace a long rectangle vertically. Trace a circle.

(5) Let the class stand and trace with their finger a long horizontal rectangle, a long vertical rectangle, and a circle.

(6) Mary, you may find a rectangle in the box and show it to the class. John and Peter may do the same.

(7) What in the room is shaped like a rectangle? Lead the pupils to see that the doors, windows, blackboard, side of the room, ceiling, etc., are rectangular in shape.

(8) You may all draw a long vertical rectangle on your tablets, and a long horizontal rectangle.

(9) Draw Fig. 7 on the blackboard, showing the cover of the box.

(10) Tell the story of the boy who cut an opening like a rectangle in the box (cut or draw the opening) and how he placed his little sister's doll in the box in such a manner as to represent her looking as through a window.

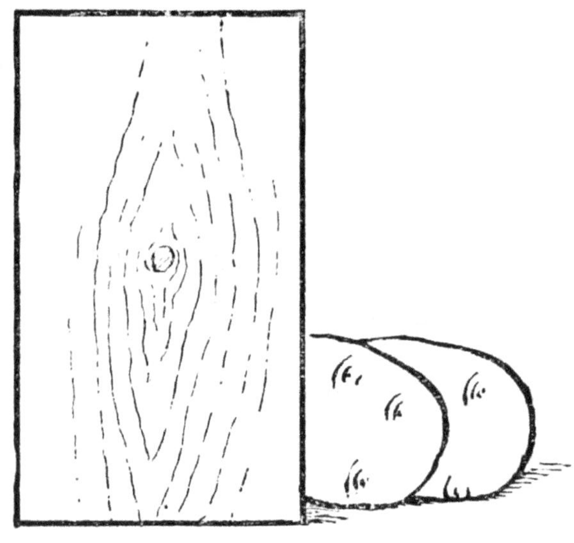

8

FIGURE 8. – (1) Place the box before the class, showing the side with a number of potatoes rolling from it.

(2) Review the rectangle.

(3) Draw the box on the blackboard, and represent the potatoes rolling out.

9

FIGURE 9. – (1) Drill the class at the blackboard with easy problems like the following:

(2) Draw a long horizontal line, a short horizontal line, a short vertical line, and a long vertical line. Draw a long horizontal rectangle, a short horizontal rectangle, a short vertical rectangle, and a long vertical rectangle.

(3) Place the box, showing the side, before the class, and place a doll inside.

(4) Draw the box on the blackboard, and in it represent a doll.

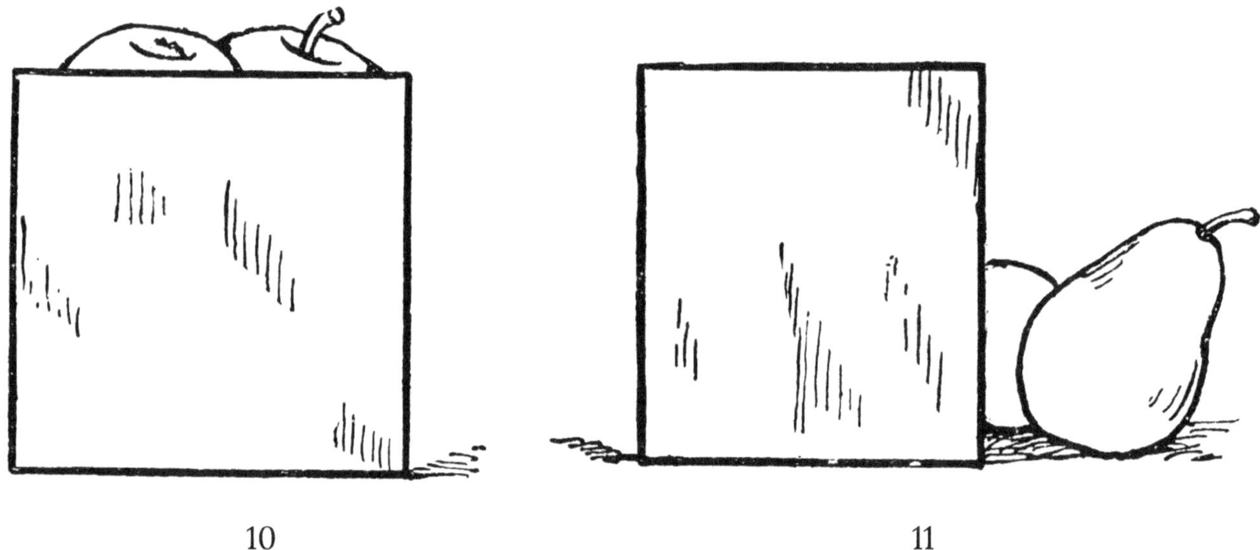

10   11

FIGURE 10. - (1) Place the box before the class and then draw it on the blackboard.

(2) Place two or more apples in the box in such a manner that they will show above the edge.

(3) Represent the apples in the drawing.

(4) Review.

FIGURE 11. - (1) Review edges, corners, faces, horizontal and vertical lines, and rectangles.

(2) Place the box before the class and then draw it on the blackboard.

(3) The object in placing the box before drawing it is to enable the class to compare the box with the drawing.

(4) Place a couple of pears as if they had rolled from the box, and represent them in the drawing.

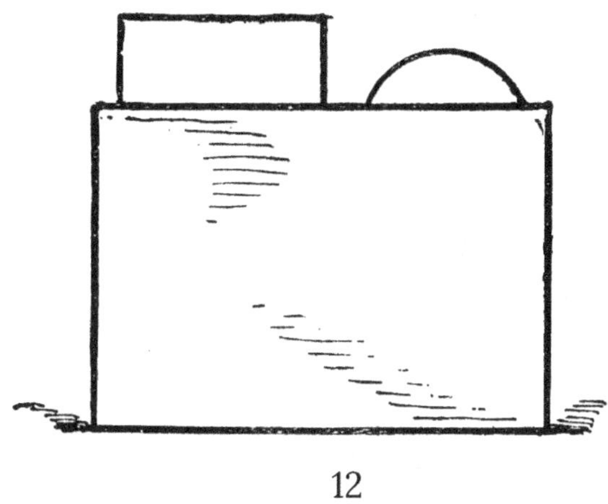

12

FIGURE 12. - (1) Place the box before the class and draw it on the blackboard.

(2) Place another box and sphere inside in such a manner that they will show above the edge.

(3) Represent them in the drawing.

(4) Let the class do likewise.

13

FIGURE 13. – (1) Place the box before the class and draw it on the blackboard.

(2) Represent a mouse on the box with its tail hanging over the edge.

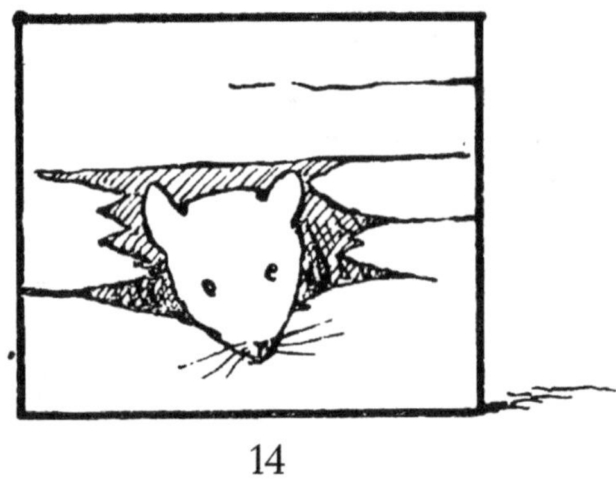

14

FIGURE 14. – (1) Place the box before the class and draw it on the blackboard.

(2) Represent the end of the box as broken.

(3) Show how a rat has converted it into a house.

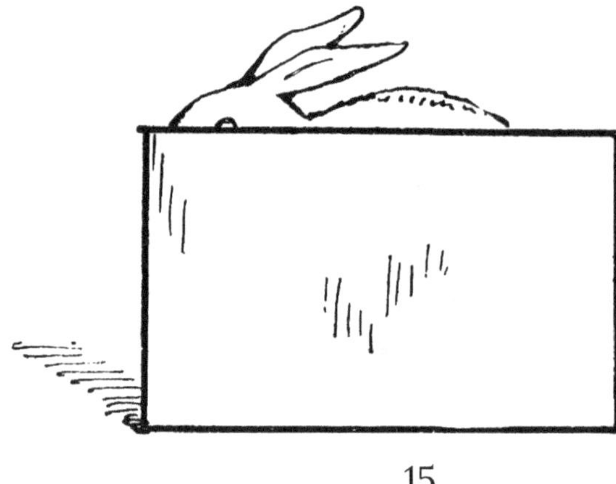

15

FIGURE 15. – (1) Draw the box on the blackboard as before.

(2) Tell the story of the rabbit that hid in the box to keep from the dog, and show how the rabbit is peeping above the edge to see if the dog has gone.

(3) Let the pupils draw these devices, but do not insist on great accuracy. Remember, you are teaching a type form, not a rabbit.

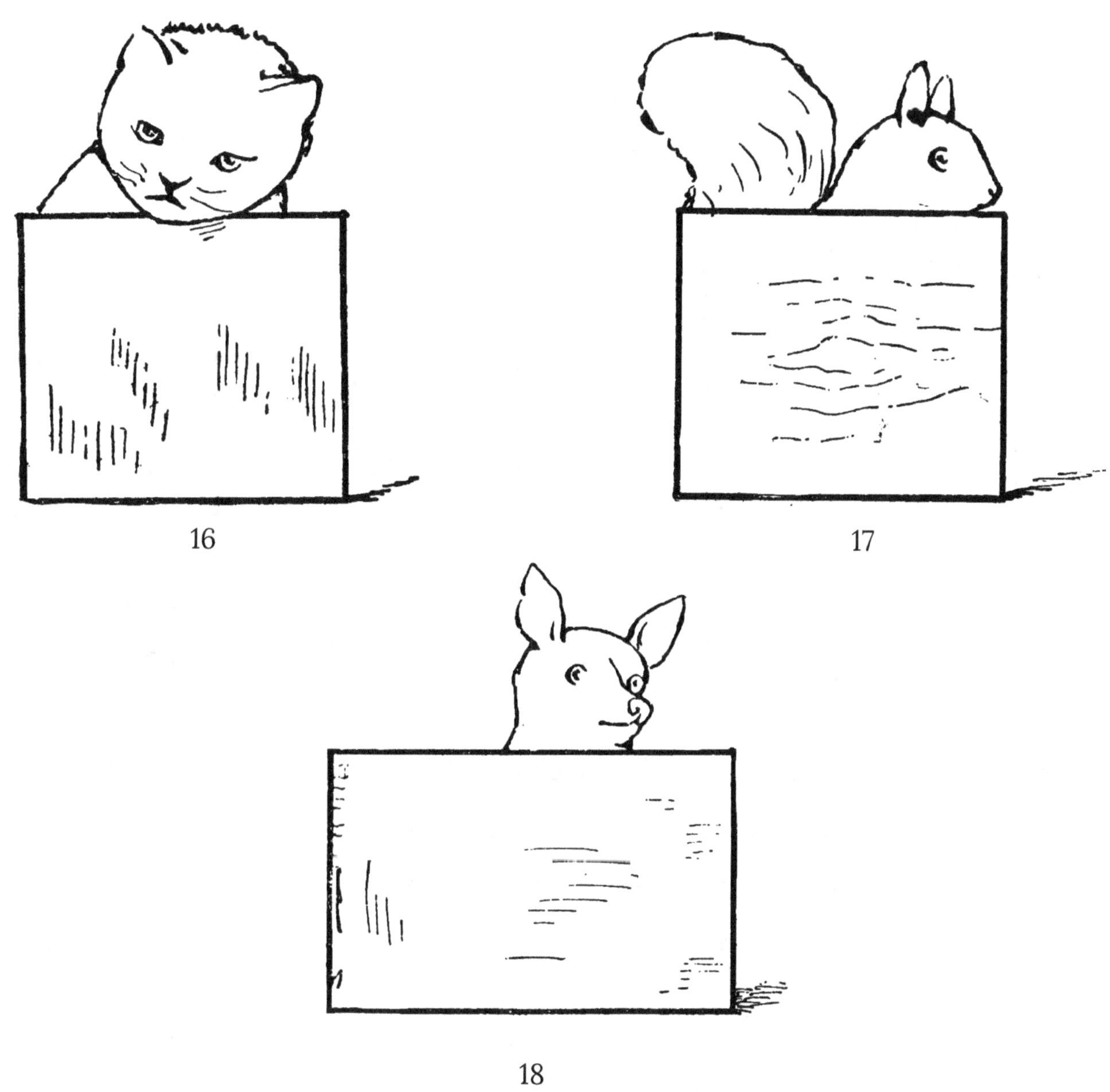

16

17

18

FIGURE 16, 17, AND 18. – Teach these figures very much like Fig. 15.

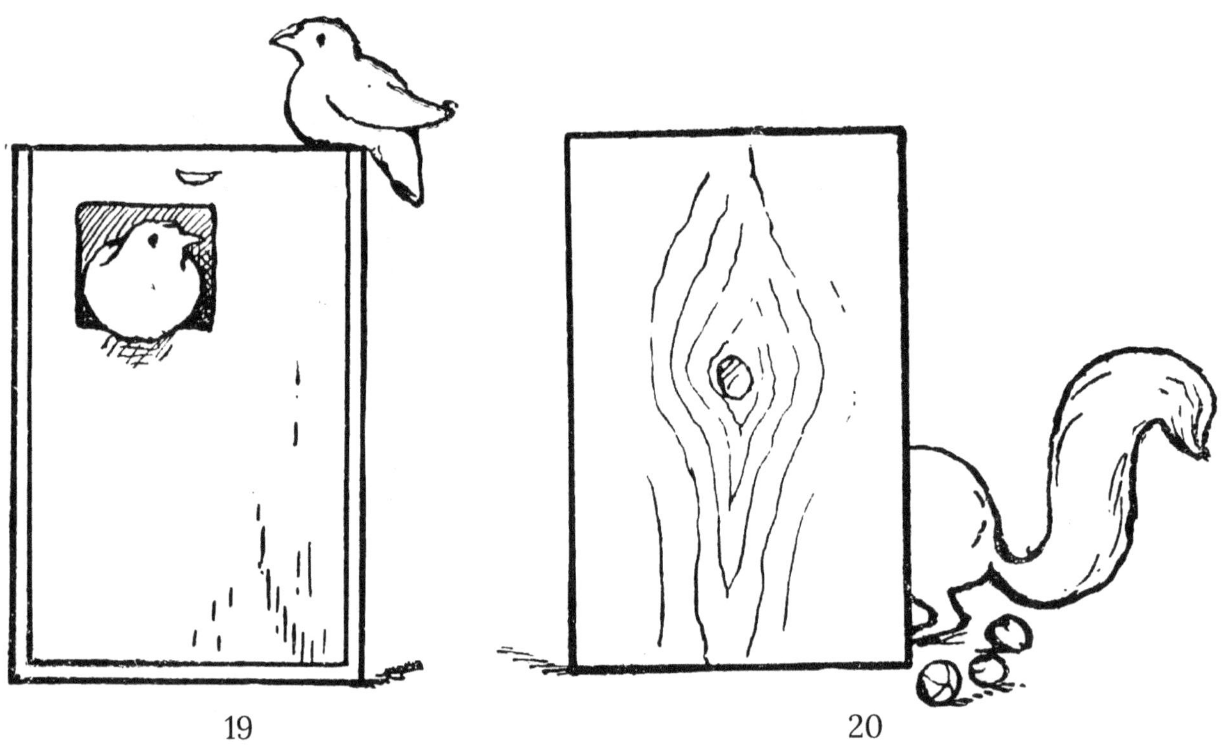

19   20

FIGURE 19. – (1) Place the box before the class and draw it on the blackboard.

(2) Tell the story of the boy who cut a rectangular opening in the cover and how two birds built their nest on the inside, using the opening as a door.

(3) Draw the opening and birds at the proper time.

FIGURE 20. – (1) Place the box before the class and draw it on the blackboard.

(2) Tell the story of how Johnny put some nuts in a box and how a squirrel discovered them, tipped over the box, and ate them up.

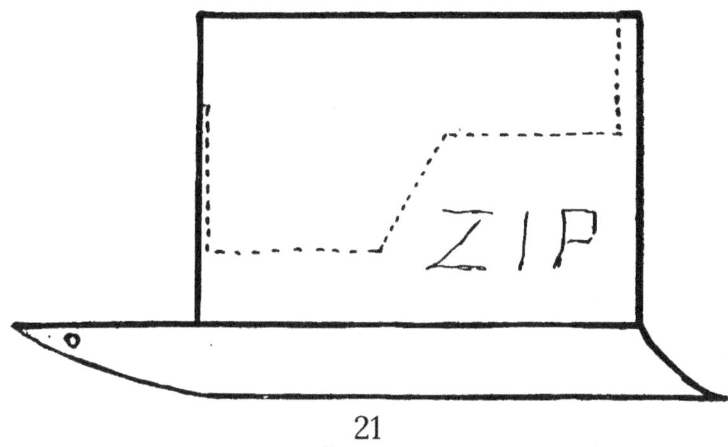

21

FIGURE 21. – (1) Place the box before the class and draw it on the blackboard.

(2) Tell how an ingenious boy put some runners on his box and made a sled of it.

(3) Tell how he cut his box down, as indicated by the dotted lines, and made it into a cutter.

22

FIGURE 22. – (1) Review with the class at the blackboard.

(2) Let each draw a box.

(3) John, you may fill your box with apples. Mary may place an apple on her box. Lucile may place an apple on each side of her box, etc., etc.

(4) Represent a box on the blackboard, and in it cut a round opening.

(5) Tell how some bees discovered the opening and built their nest in it.

(6) Represent the bees flying about.

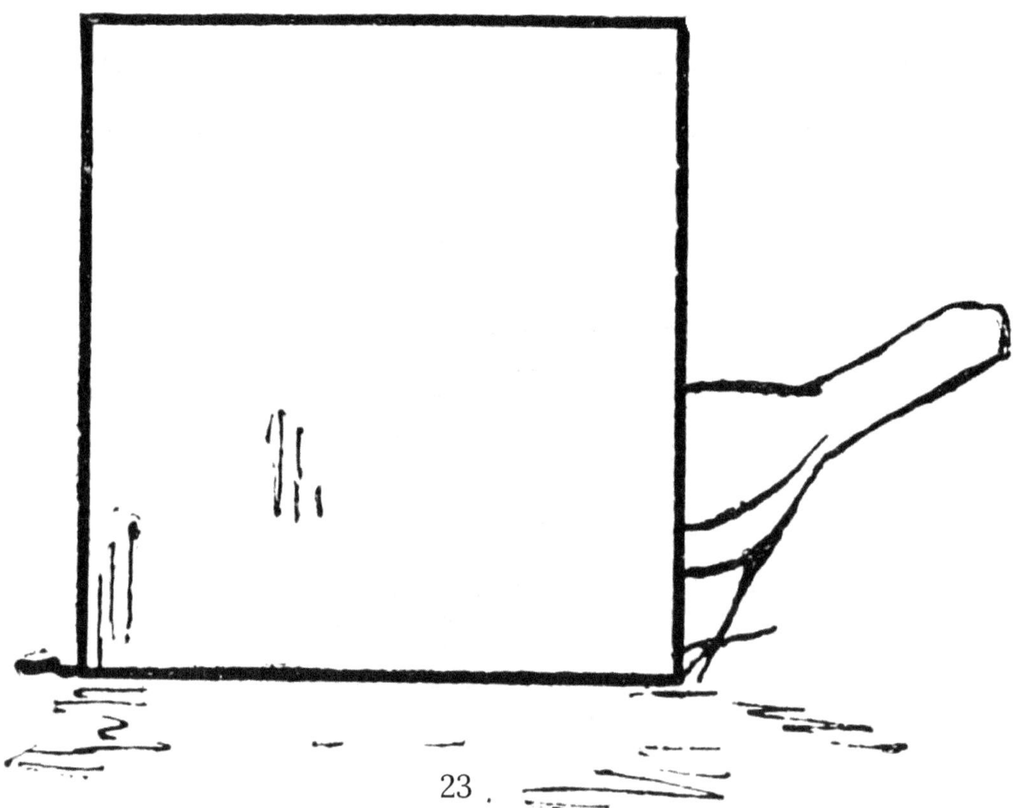

FIGURE 23. – (1) Draw a box on the blackboard and represent a bird part way in the open side.

FIGURE 24. – (1) Place the box before the class and draw it on the blackboard.

(2) Tell the story of the boy who put some wheels on his box and turned it into a little wagon. How he lost his wagon, and when he found it, an old bird had built her nest in it and was in full possession.

APPLICATION OF THE BOX TO SIMILAR FORMS

One of the most important points in drawing is to show the relation and application of the box to other forms similar in shape but differing in size and details. To show that the shape of the box or one of its faces is the same as the window, door, ceiling, floor, etc., etc.

This can be taught easily and effectively by:

(1) Drawing the box on the blackboard.

(2) Changing the box into the object it resembles.

Some of the most common objects similar in shape to the box, and drawn by the same principles, are boxes, bins, chests, trunks, baskets, books, bookcases, desks, tables, chairs, bureaus, beds, stands, safes, stools, stones, houses, barns, sheds, shanties, cabins, rooms, halls, stairs, chimneys, windows, doors, pens, fences, walls, gates, bars, fenced fields, roads, walks, streets, bridges, wharves, wagons, tunnels, cars, lumber piles, etc., etc.

25

FIGURE 25. – (1) Draw the end of the crayon box on the blackboard.

(2) Turn it into a pasteboard box by adding a cover.

(3) Print on the box "Best Candy."

(4) Tell the story of the boy who could not procure a pumpkin to make a jack-o'-lantern, so made one out of a candy box by cutting in the eyes, nose, and mouth, and placing a bit of candle inside for the light.

26

FIGURE 26. – (1) Draw the end of the box on the blackboard.

(2) Call attention to the fact that an open space has shape as well as an object. Open the window and compare the end of the box with the open space. Open the door and compare the open space with the side of the box.

(3) Open the door and let the class choose the side of the box that most nearly resembles the open space. In like manner, let them compare the open transom, open gate, etc., with dif-

ferent sides of the box.

(4) Turn the end of the box drawn on the board into an opening and in it represent a couple of doves.

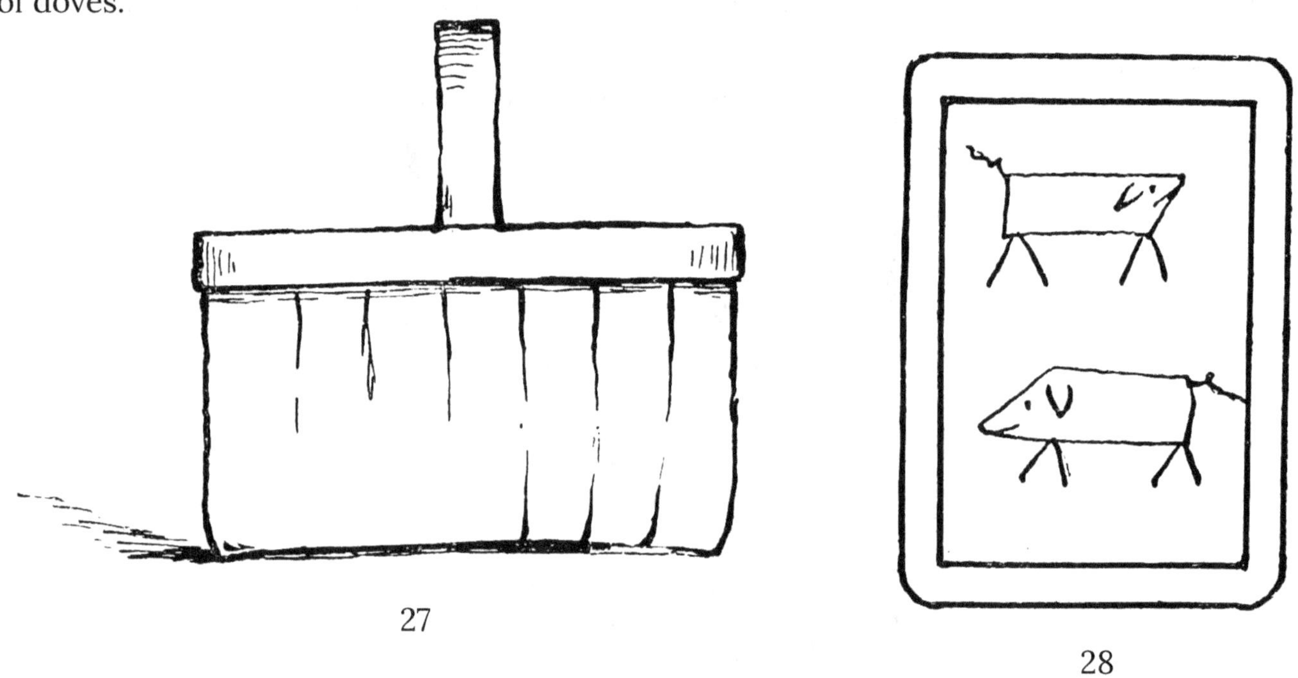

27

28

FIGURE 27. – (1) Hold a face of the box toward the class and ask them to pick out some object or space in the room similar to it.

(2) Point to some object or space in the room, such as the blackboard, ceiling, side of the room, etc., and let the class choose the face of the box that most nearly represents it.

(3) Practice these exercises often.

(4) Draw the side of the box on the blackboard and turn it into a basket.

(5) Fill the basket with apples, pears, or other familiar objects.

 FIGURE 28. – (1) Hold a slate up before the class and compare it with the face of the box that it most nearly resembles.

(2) Draw the box on the blackboard.

(3) Turn it into a slate.

(4) Draw a picture on the slate.

29

FIGURE 29. – (1) Place the side of the box before the class and draw it on the blackboard.

(2) Turn it into a cage.

(3) Represent a lion or other animal in the cage.

30

FIGURE 30. – (1) Draw the side of the box on the blackboard.

(2) Turn it into a squirrel cage.

(3) Represent a squirrel in the cage.

FIGURE 31. – (1) Ask a pupil which side of the box most nearly resembles the door. The side that he chooses, draw on the blackboard.

(2) Turn it into a door.

(3) Represent a hole in the door for kitty to go in and out.

(4) Show how someone has put his drawing lesson on the door.

32

FIGURE 32. – (1) Let a member of the class choose the face of the box that most nearly re-sembles a window.

(2) Draw this face on the blackboard.

(3) Turn it into a window.

(4) Susie, you may take the pointer and point to as many rectangles in the window as you can find.

(5) Represent the cat asleep in the window, and the dog inclined to play with her.

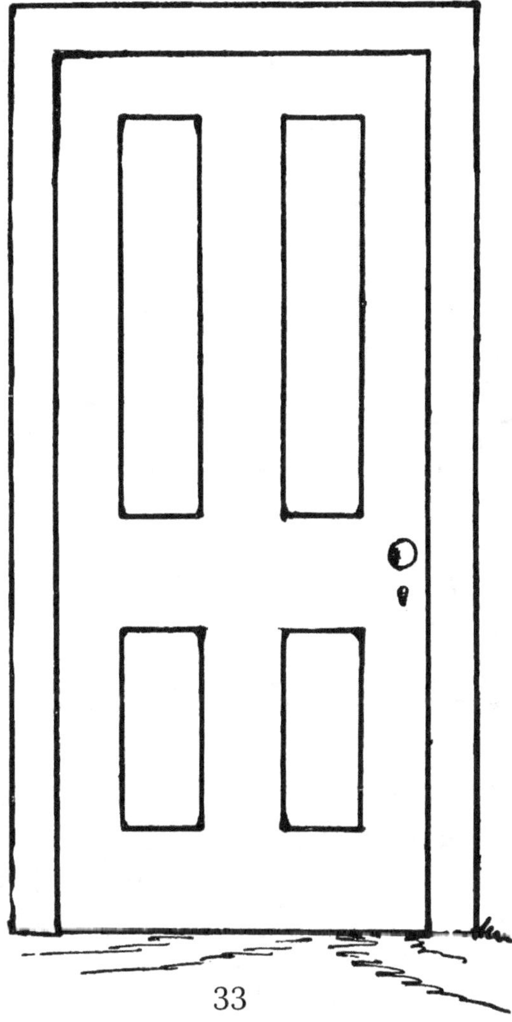

33

FIGURE 33. – (1) Give the crayon box to a pupil and ask him to choose the face of the box that most nearly resembles the door.

(2) Draw the face of the box on the blackboard.

(3) Turn it into a door.

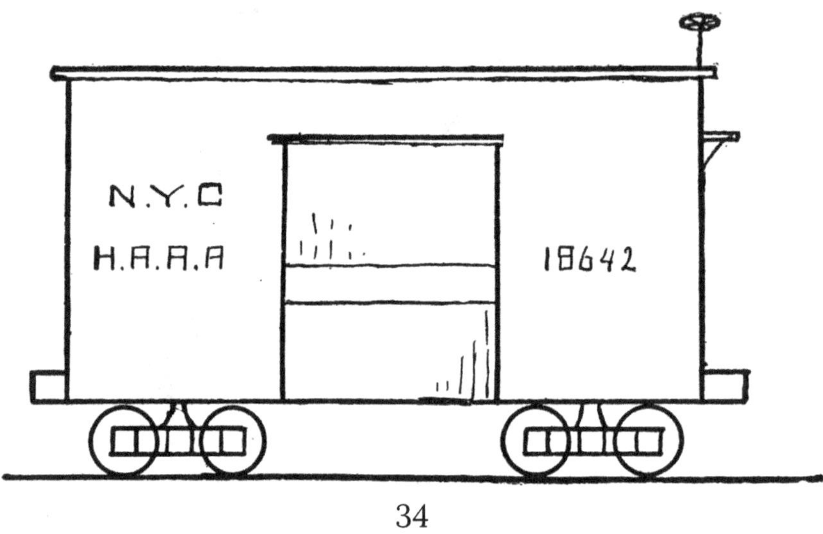

34

FIGURE 34. – (1) Draw the side of the box on the blackboard.

(2) Turn it into a freight car.

35

FIGURE 35. – (1) Draw the side of the crayon box on the black-board. (2) Turn it into a hen

house. (3) Show how someone has used the side of the house for a black-board.

FIGURE 36. – (1) Draw the side of the crayon box on the black-board.

(2) Bisect the line AB and from it, draw a vertical line as high as the point C is to be.

(3) Draw AC and BC.

(4) Ask the class what the drawing resembles. A chorus of answers will be given: a house, a barn, etc. The teacher thinks it looks like a house.

(5) Let the pupils tell you how to finish the house. You ask, "What do you need to finish our house?" Another chorus of answers: "A door, a window, a chimney, etc."

You will choose from their answers. For example, you choose a door.

Where shall we place the door? How large shall we make it?" Ask such questions as will lead the pupils to put the door, or whatever you are talking about, in the right place and of the right size.

(6) In like manner, lead the class to suggest whatever you have in mind, or have prepared for the lesson.

(7) Let the pupils draw on their tablets as rapidly as you do on the black-board.

(8) Ask some member of the class to take the crayon box and to choose the face that most resembles the door, window, chimney, etc.

FIGURE 37 AND 38. – (1) Draw the end of the crayon box twice, and the side once, on the black-board. (2) Turn one end into a gate, the other into the fence between the gate and bars, and the side into bars.

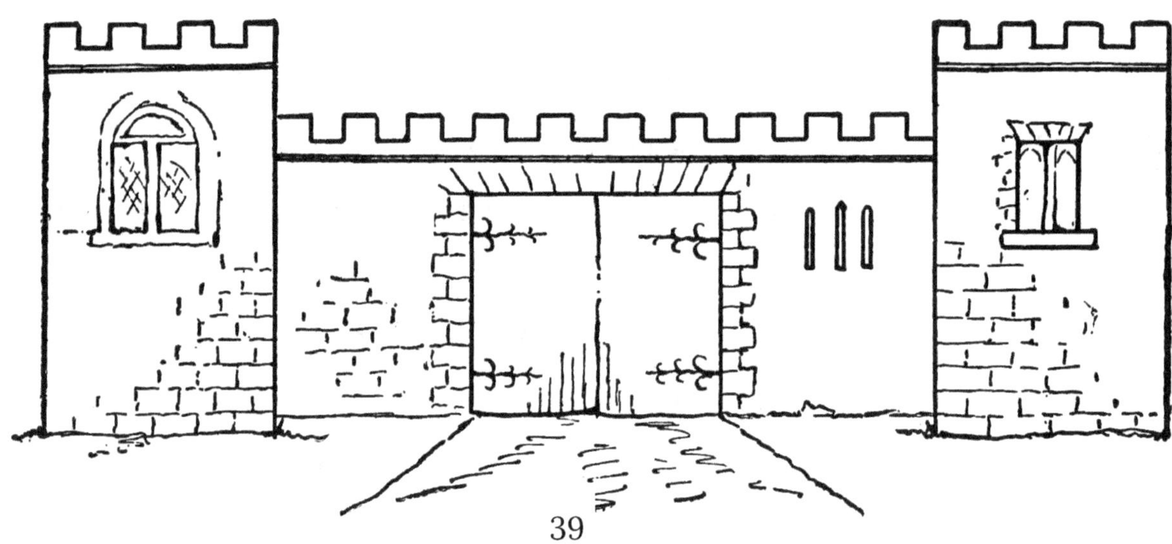

39

FIGURE 39. – (1) Draw the side of the crayon box on the blackboard and at each end draw the same in a vertical position. Draw the end in the center for the doors.

(2) Turn them into a castle.

(3) Drill on the different forms that compose the different parts of the castle.

WHEN TWO FACES OF THE CUBE ARE SEEN.

Use for a model a cube, or better still, a cubical pasteboard box.

UNDER THIS HEAD TEACH THE SQUARE.

(1) Hold a cube or a square form before the class.

(2) Lead them to see that the vertical and horizontal edges are equal.

(3) Compare a square with a rectangle.

(4) George may choose a square from the box of figures and hold it up before the class.

Choose a square and rectangle and hold them up before the class.

(5) See who can find a square in the room.

(6) Draw a square and a rectangle on the blackboard and ask questions of comparison.

(7) Let the class draw a square on their tablets. A rectangle.

(8) Drill the class at the blackboard on problems similar to the following: Draw a square.

Draw a vertical rectangle (Fig. 8). Draw a horizontal rectangle (Fig. 3). Draw a long horizontal

rectangle. A short horizontal rectangle. Draw a square and a short vertical rectangle, etc.

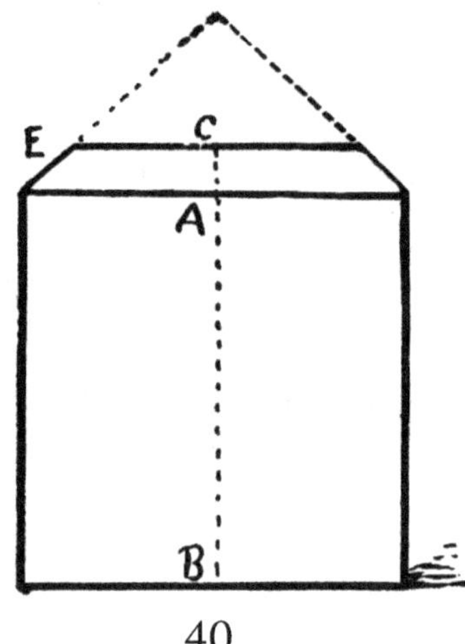

40

FIGURE 40. – (1) Place the cube in such a manner as to show the front and top faces.

(2) Draw the front face on the blackboard.

(3) Choose a center of vision and to it draw receding lines.

(4) Choose the point E and finish the cube.

(5) Let the class draw a similar one.

(6) Do not explain the center of vision or the receding lines at this time, but trust to the strong perceptive powers of the child.

(7) Let the class draw the cube several times. Each one will represent the receding face too long. Be very patient at this point, and lead the pupils to see how narrow the receding face is as compared with the front face. Measure the distance A B in the drawing and compare it with A C, and let the pupils do the same.

(8) Practice will usually correct this fault.

(9) Teach the pupils to be guided by the appearance.

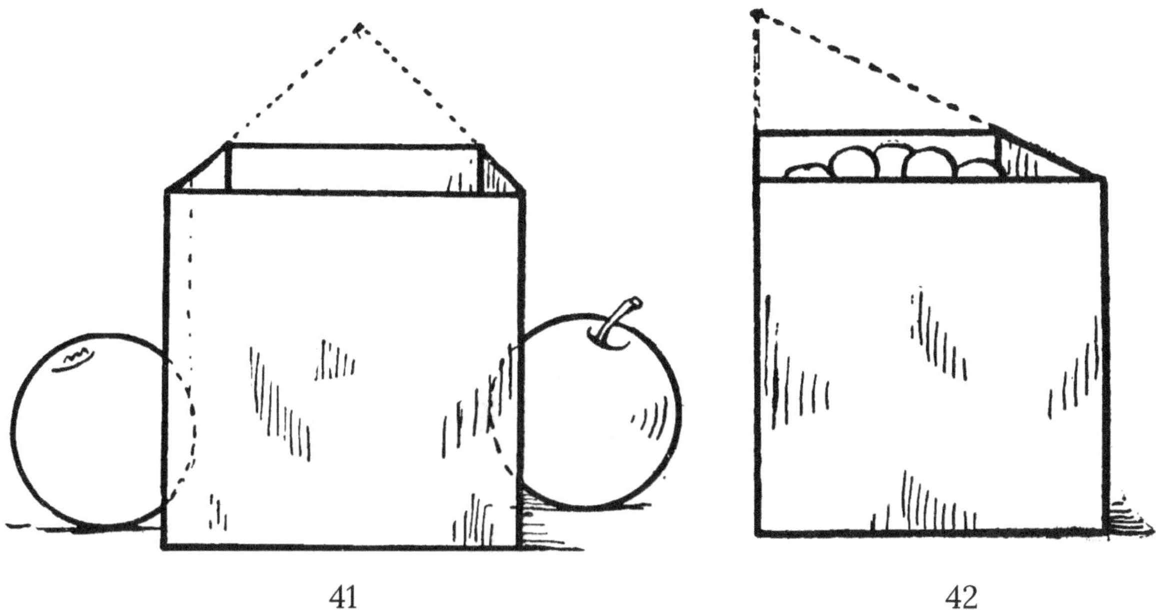

41   42

FIGURE 41. – (1) Place the cube or box before the class as in Fig. 40 and draw it on the blackboard in the same manner.

(2) Represent the cube as an empty box by drawing two vertical lines from the further corners. Place a box before the class and let them see these lines.

(3) Let the class draw a similar cube.

(4) Place an apple on each side of the cube and represent similar ones in the drawing.

FIGURE 42. – (1) Place the cube before the class as in Fig. 40 and draw it on the blackboard.

(2) Place the center of vision over the left corner of the cube and draw it. Erase and place the center of vision over the right corner, and draw as before.

(3) Do this several times to show that the center of vision is not confined to one place.

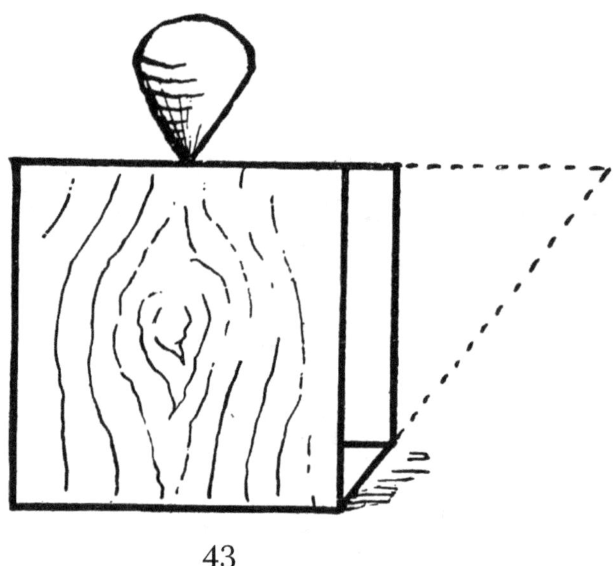

43

FIGURE 43. – (1) Place the cube before the class in such a manner as to show the front and a side face.

(2) Draw a square on the blackboard. Place the center of vision at the right of the upper corner and draw the cube. Erase and place the point at the right of the lower corner and draw as before.

(3) Place the center of vision at the right in various places to show that it is not confined to one place.

(4) Represent the cube with the side off.

(5) Let the pupils make similar drawings in each position of the center of vision.

(6) Drill with the class at the blackboard. Let each pupil draw a square. With crayon in hand, mark a center of vision at the right of each and let the pupil finish the cube.

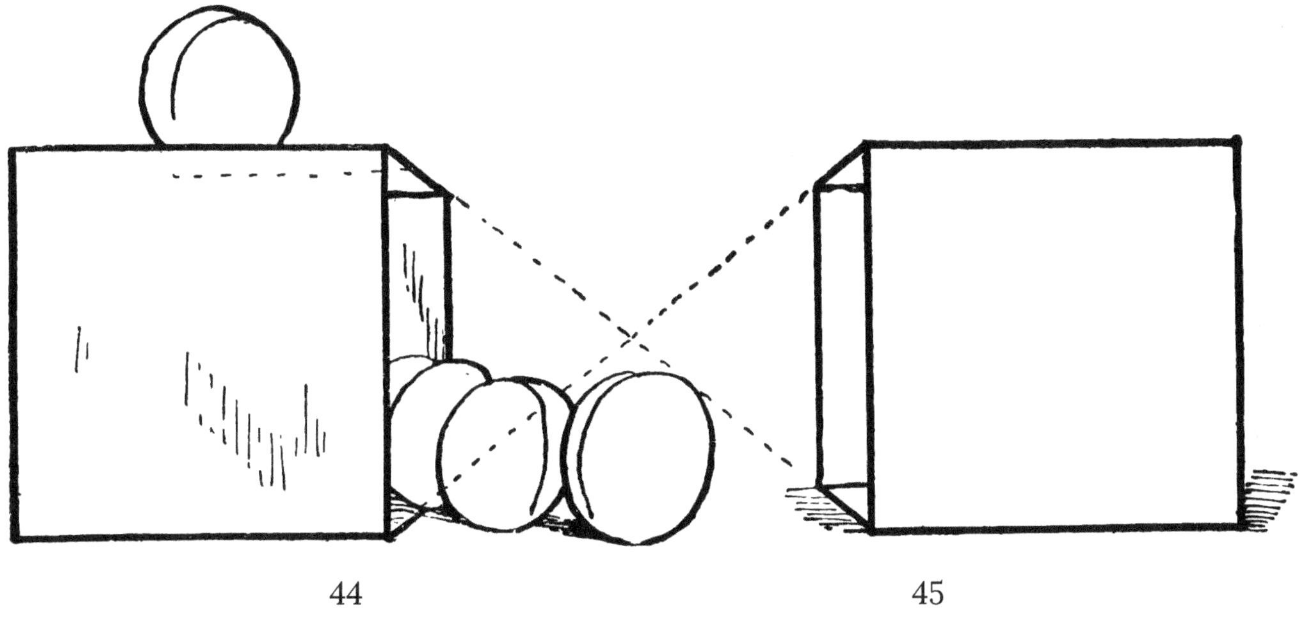

44   45

FIGURE 44 AND 45. – (1) Place two cubes before the class so as to show the right and front face of one and the left and front face of the other.

(2) Draw them on the blackboard in this position, using one center of vision for both.

(3) Represent the cubes as empty boxes by removing the sides.

(4) Place some peaches or other round objects rolling from the boxes.

WHEN THREE OR MORE SIDES OF THE CUBE ARE SEEN.

Any of the devices used with the sphere or in Fig. 1 - 39 may be used in this part.

UNDER THIS HEAD TEACH:

(1) Receding lines.

(2) Parallel lines.

(3) Surfaces.

(4) Center of vision.

(5) Horizon line.

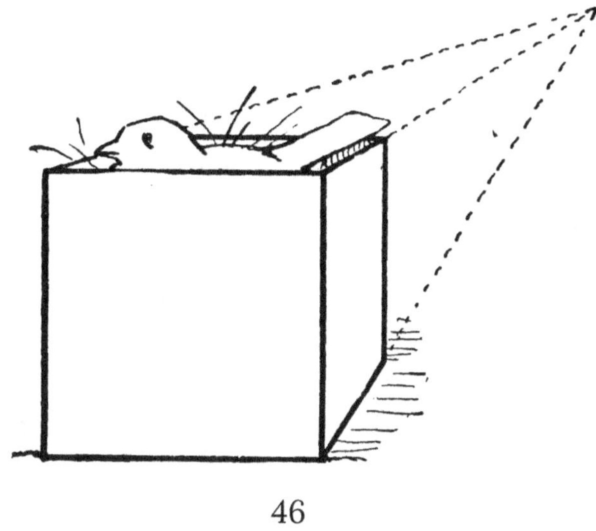

46

RECEDING LINES.

FIGURE 46. – (1) Place the cube before the class in such a manner as to show three faces.

(2) Draw it in this position on the blackboard.

(3) Mary may take the pointer and point to each vertical edge on the box. Each vertical line in the drawing. Each horizontal line in the drawing. Each horizontal edge on the box.

(4) Joseph may take the pointer and point to a vertical edge on the box, and then to the line that corresponds to it in the drawing. Point to a horizontal line in the drawing and to the edge that corresponds to it on the box.

(5) Nellie may take the pointer and point to each vertical edge. To each horizontal edge. To an edge that is neither vertical nor horizontal. Nellie will probably point to a receding edge.

(6) Teach the name *receding edge*. Teach that the receding edge is one that runs *away from*

you, that it is the runaway edge.

(7) Hold the pointer vertical, oblique, horizontal, receding, and lead the class to recognize each position. A recognition of the oblique line may be taught at this point but no more.

(8) George may take the pointer and hold it vertical, oblique, horizontal, receding.

(9) All may find a horizontal edge on their desks. A receding edge. Find a vertical edge in the room; a receding edge.

(10) Eloise may take the pointer and point to the receding lines in the drawing. Point to a receding edge on the box and the same receding line in the drawing.

(11) Class may make a similar drawing to the one on the blackboard.

(12) Turn the cube into a box.

(13) Represent a bird on her nest in the box, with an appropriate story.

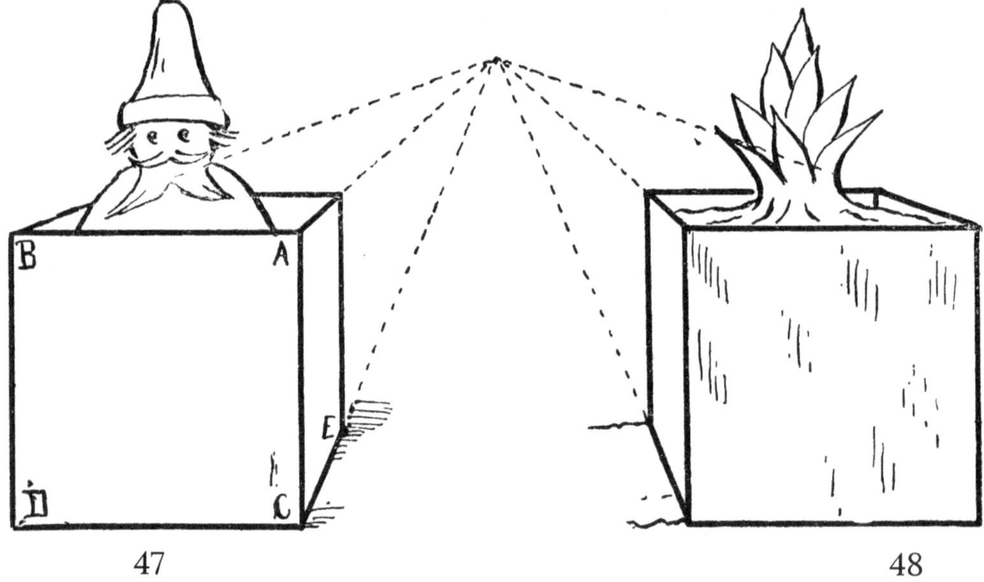

FIGURE 47. – (1) Place the cube in position and draw it on the blackboard.

(2) Drill as in Fig. 46.

(3) Lead the class to see that each corner is formed by three lines: a vertical, a horizontal, and a receding.

(4) Point to corner A and ask how many lines can be seen. How many kinds of lines? How many kinds of lines can be seen at corner B? At corner C? At corner D? What line is lacking at corner D? Why can it not be seen? How many lines can be seen at corner E? Where is the third line?

(5) Drill on the real cube in the same manner.

(6) Drill the class by letting them point out the different edges on the cube and corresponding lines in the drawing, and vice versa.

FIGURE 48. – (1) Place the cube in position before the class and draw it on the blackboard.

(2) Drill with the class at the blackboard.

(3) Let each pupil draw a square on the board.

(4) With crayon in hand, mark a center of vision somewhere around each square and let the pupil finish the cube.

FIGURE 47 AND 48. – (1) Place two cubes before the class, one below and at the right, one below and at the left of the eye, and draw them on the blackboard.

(2) Drill on the receding lines and corners.

(3) Represent the cubes as empty boxes.

(4) In one, draw a Jack-in-the-box and in the other a plant.

(5) Let the class make similar drawings.

PARALLEL LINES.

Teach (1) vertical parallel lines, (2) horizontal parallel lines, (3) receding parallel lines.

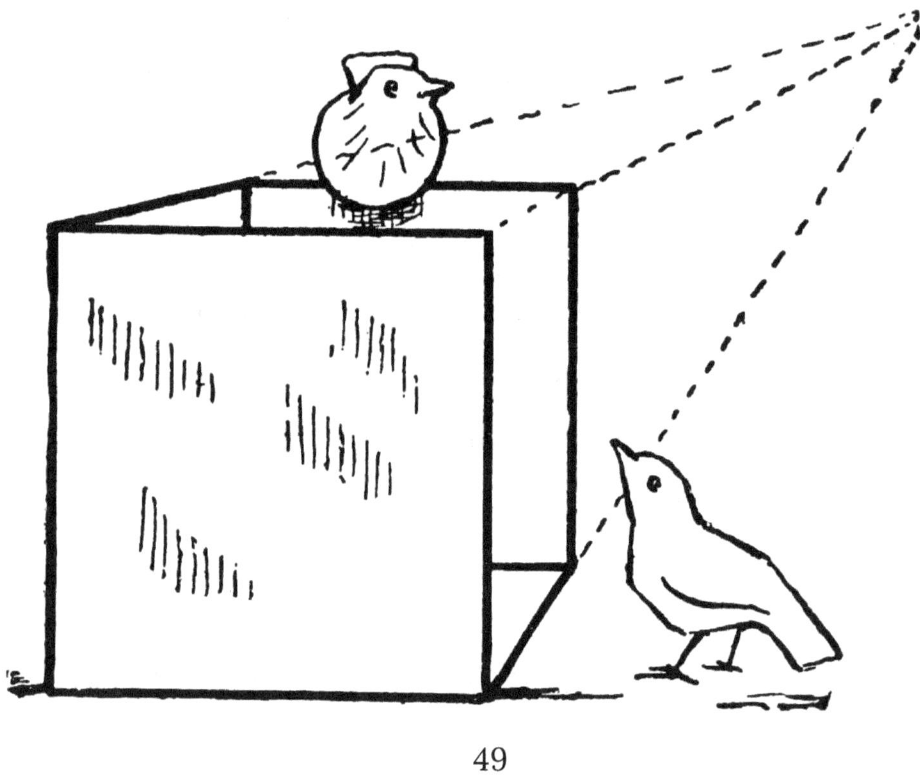

49

FIGURE 49. – (1) Place the cube before the class and draw it on the blackboard.

(2) Teach parallel lines.

(3) Hold a pointer in each hand and lead the class to see that when they are the same distance apart all the way, they are parallel. Point to parallel edges in the room. Draw parallel lines on the blackboard.

(4) Hold the pointers vertical for vertical parallel lines, horizontal for horizontal parallel lines, and receding for receding parallel lines, and teach the class to recognize each kind. (There is no objection to teaching oblique parallel lines at this point, but do not teach oblique receding lines.)

(5) Harry may take the pointers and hold them so as to represent vertical parallel lines, horizontal parallel lines, receding parallel lines.

(6) Marie may take the pointer and point to vertical parallel lines in the drawing; to horizontal parallel lines; to receding parallel lines. Point to vertical, horizontal, and receding parallel edges on the cube.

(7) Walter may find two or more vertical parallel edges in the room. Nellie, two or more horizontal parallel edges; Lottie, two or more receding parallel edges.

(8) All may draw a cube and mark the vertical parallel lines "a," the horizontal parallel lines "b," and the receding parallel lines "c."

(9) Represent the cube as a box by removing the top face.

(10) Remove the side face.

(11) Tell how two birds are looking for a place to build their nest. (Draw the birds.)

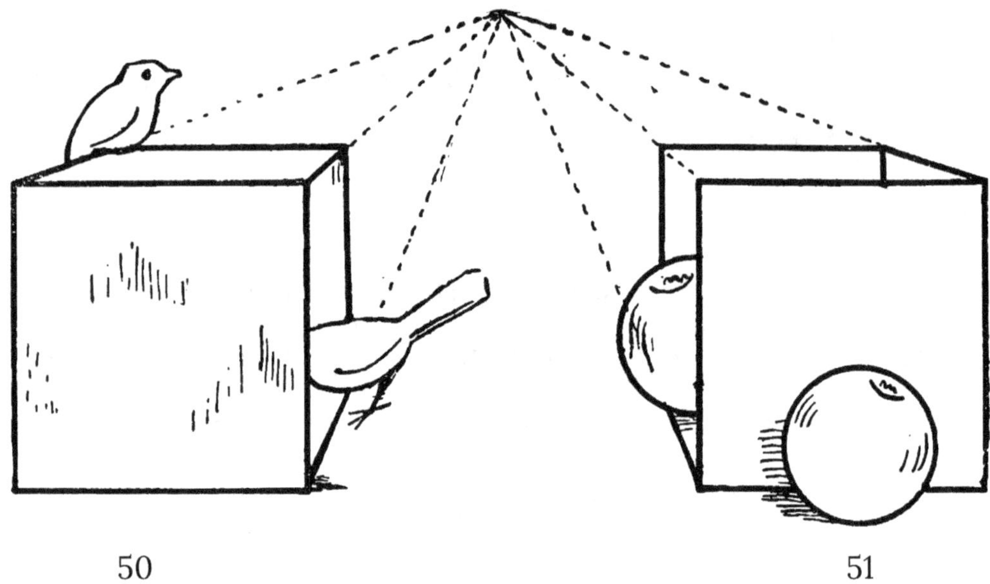

50   51

FIGURE 50. – (1) Place the cube before the class and draw it on the blackboard.

(2) Review the three classes of parallel lines thoroughly by letting the pupils point to them on the cube, and then to the corresponding ones in the drawing.

(3) Remove one side of the cube and represent the two birds still searching for a place to build their nest.

SURFACES.

Teach the (1) vertical face or surface.

(2) Vertical receding face or surface.

(3) Horizontal receding face or surface.

The horizontal surface is not seen in drawing.

Procure a square or rectangular piece of pasteboard or similar substance.

(2) Hold it vertically before the class and teach the vertical face or surface. Hold it in a vertical receding position and teach the vertical receding surface. Hold it horizontally before the class and teach the horizontal receding surface.

(3) John may take the board and hold it so it represents a vertical surface, a vertical receding surface, and a horizontal receding surface.

(4) Mary may find a vertical surface in the room. James, a vertical receding surface. Lucy, a horizontal receding surface.

FIGURE 51. – (1) Hold a cube before the class and point to a vertical face, a vertical receding face, a horizontal receding face, and see if they recognize each.

(2) Draw the cube on the blackboard.

(3) James may take the pointer and point to a vertical face, a horizontal receding face, a vertical receding face in the drawing.

(4) Lucile may take the pointer and point to a vertical face on the cube, and the corresponding vertical face in the drawing. The same with the horizontal and vertical receding faces.

(5) The signs, Figs. 75, 76, and 77, represent vertical, horizontal receding, and vertical receding faces, and may be used to explain these surfaces.

52

53

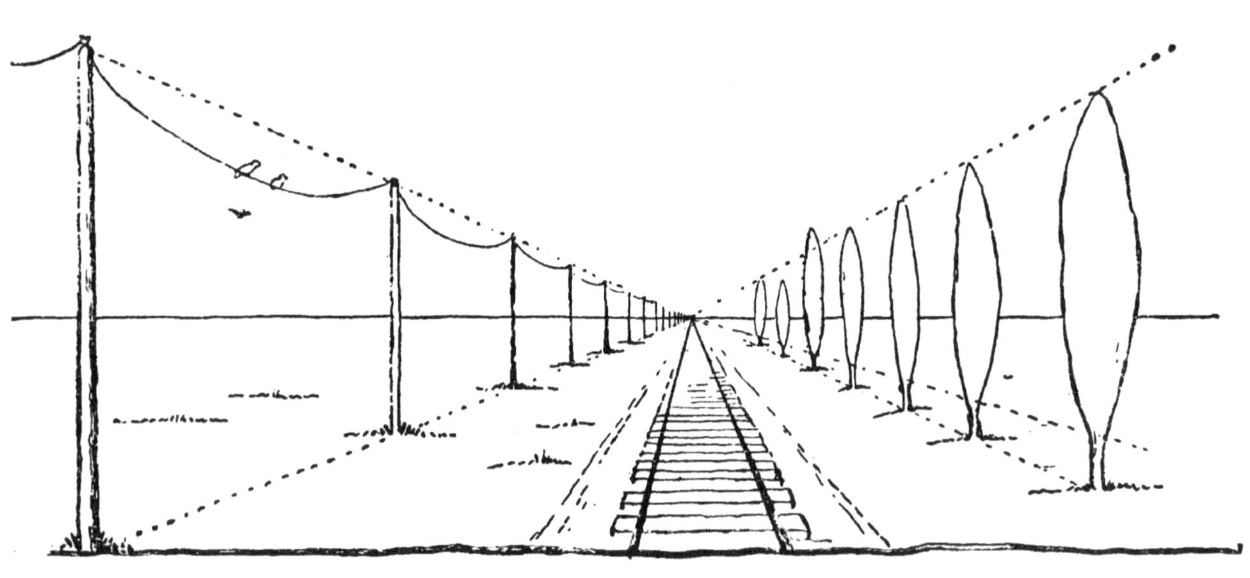

54

THE CENTER OF VISION.

The Center of Vision is the imaginary point in the horizon line directly opposite the eye. It cannot be seen in nature, but its position may be placed by observation, and in the drawing, it may be marked. The center of vision is very much like the North Pole: not visible to the eye, but very essential in drawing, as the pole is in geography.

All receding lines that are at right angles with horizontal and vertical lines vanish at the center of vision.

The center of vision may be taught as follows:

FIGURE 54. – (1) Place on the blackboard a picture similar to Fig. 54.

(2) Ask the pupils if they ever noticed how the rails of a railroad seemed to come together, or how the fences and sides of any straight road seemed to converge. All have noticed this. If not, take the class out in the street or road and show them that this is so.

(3) In the row of trees, ask which is the tallest? Lead the class to see that trees are of the same height when they touch the same parallel lines. That the fifth tree is the tallest, and the sixth tree is the shortest in the row. That the reason the further trees look smaller is that they are farther away.

(4) Let a pupil walk away and let the class notice that he grows smaller the further he goes away.

(5) Lizzie may take the pointer and point to some vertical parallel lines in the picture; horizontal parallel lines; receding parallel lines; to the tallest tree, the shortest tree; to the trees that are of the same height.

(6) Lead the pupils to see that all the receding lines vanish at the center of vision.

(7) Teach that the center of vision is opposite the eye. Point directly in front of the eye for your center of vision and teach the class to point to theirs in the same manner.

(8) Teach that all the receding lines vanishing at the center of vision are parallel.

(9) When a point is explained in the schoolroom, try and show the same point outdoors, in nature.

LEVEL OF THE EYE.

The horizon line is the line that marks the level of the eye. Unlike the center of vision, it can be seen on the coast, or in a level country, Fig. 52. It is the line where the earth and sky seem to meet.

The level of the eye is a trifle above this line, but for all practical purposes, they are the same.

The horizon line should be taught as the line that represents the level of the eye. It is by far the most important line in the picture and determines the drawing of all receding lines.

It is a good idea to call this line the *level of the eye line.*

The center of vision is always in the horizon line.

In a mountainous or hilly country, the horizon line is shut from view by the intervening mountains or hills, as in Fig. 53.

Teach the level of the eye: (1) Hold the pointer horizontally below the eye, above the eye, on a level with the eye, and teach the class to recognize each position.

(2) James may take the pointer and hold it horizontally on a level with the eye. Below the eye. Above the eye.

(3) All may hold their hand on a level with the eye. Above the eye. Below the eye.

(4) Mary may point to some object above the level of her eye. Below the level of her eye. On a level with her eye.

(5) Each may go to the blackboard and draw a horizontal line on a level with the eye. Above the eye. Below the eye.

(6) Hold the box above the level of the eyes of the class and ask if they can see the top face. Bottom face. Lead the class to see that when the box is above the eye, the bottom can be seen, but not the top. When below the eye, the top can be seen, but not the bottom, and when on a level with the eye, neither top nor bottom can be seen.

FIGURE 52 AND 53. – (1) Draw the landscape on the blackboard.

(2) Ask the class if they have ever seen a level plain, or been on the coast, and if they have

noticed the long line where the sky and earth seemed to meet. Tell them this is the horizon line and that it represents the level of the eye.

(3) Often, this line that marks the level of the eye cannot be seen because of hills and mountains being in the way. You can show how this is so by representing some mountains as in Fig. 53.

FIGURE 54. – (1) Draw a long horizontal line and, in this line, place the center of vision.

(2) Tell the class that the center of vision is always in this line.

(3) Show how the receding lines above the horizon line slant downward; how the receding lines below this line slant upward.

(4) Show this to the class outdoors by pointing to receding lines on buildings or on a real telegraph line. This may also be shown very plainly in a long hall.

(5) Drill the class as follows: William may take the pointer and point to the level of the eye in the picture. To the center of vision. What does the center of vision represent? What does the horizon line represent? What line represents the level of the eye? Point to receding lines that slant upward. Downward. When do receding lines slant upward? Downward?

(6) Let the pupils make a similar drawing.

55

FIGURE 55. – (1) Draw a horizon line and several trees to suggest a landscape.

(2) Draw the front face of the four posts.

(3) Place the center of vision.

(4) Drill the class as follows : Beginning with the post on the right ask; When this post or box is finished, could you see the top? Why? Could you see the left face? Could you see the top of the second post? Which side could be seen? Why ? Could you see either side of the third post? Why ? Could you see the top? Why? What faces of the fourth post could be seen?

(5) Lead the class to see that when the receding line is on a level with the eye, as in the second post, that it is horizontal.

(6) Drill on the level of the eye and the center of vision.

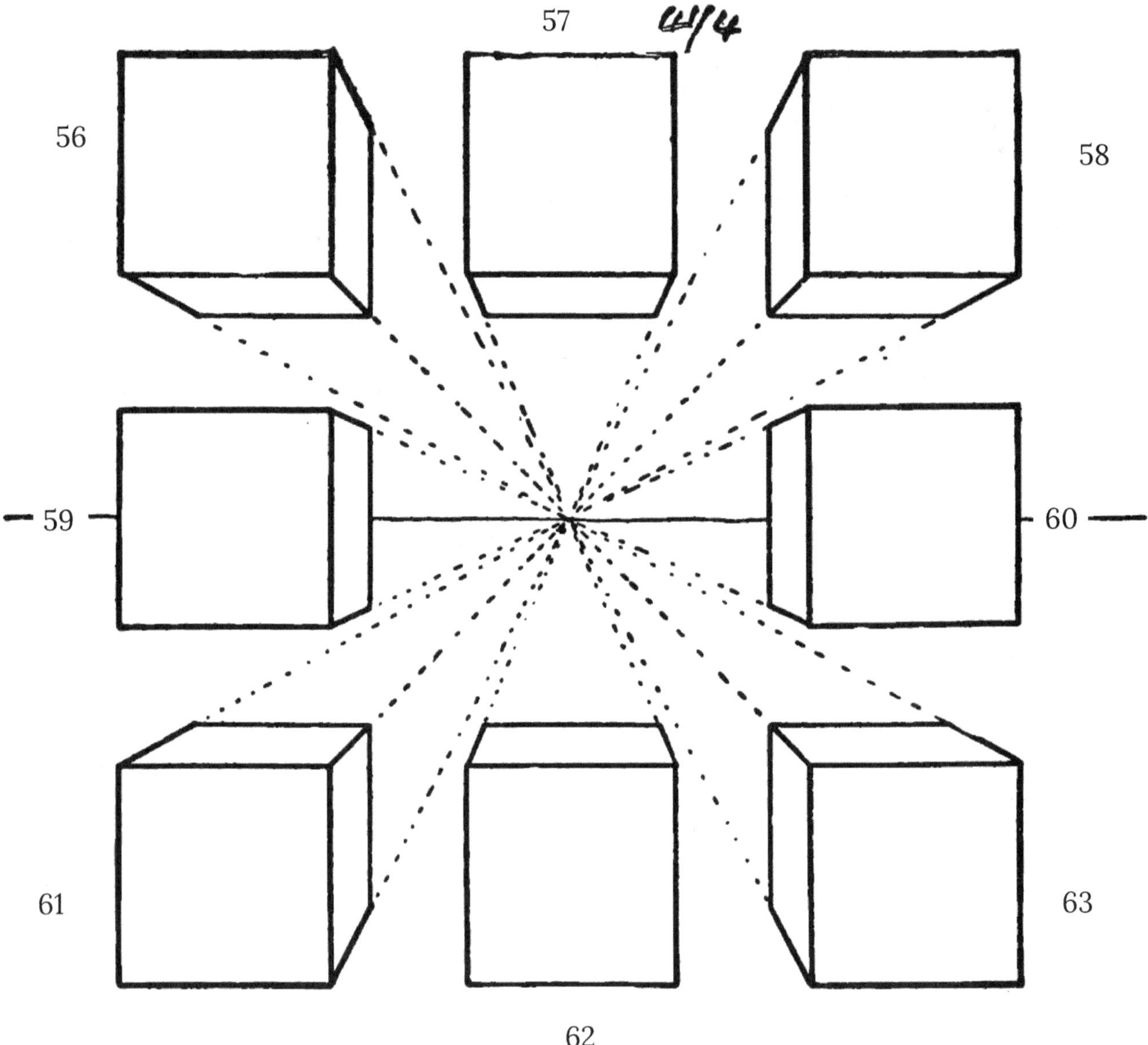

56
57
58
59
60
61
62
63

FIGURE 56 - 63. – (1) Teach the eight positions of the cube: Below the eye, Fig. 62. Above the eye, Fig. 57. At the right of the eye, Fig. 60. At the left of the eye, Fig. 59. Below and at the left of the eye, Fig. 61. Below and at the right, Fig. 63. Above and at the left, Fig. 56. Above and at the right, Fig. 58. There are nine positions. The one directly opposite the eye is omitted.

(2) Draw a long horizon line on the blackboard and, in it, place the center of vision.

(3) Hold a cube with one face flat against the blackboard in each of the above positions and let the class tell you where it is in regard to the eye (center of vision).

(4) Drill several in the class by letting each take the cube and hold it in each of the above positions.

(5) Anna may take the box and hold it below her eye. Above, etc.

(6) Draw the box in each one of these positions.

(7) Drill the class at the blackboard. Charles may draw a cube below and at the left of the eye. Anna may draw one above the eye, etc.

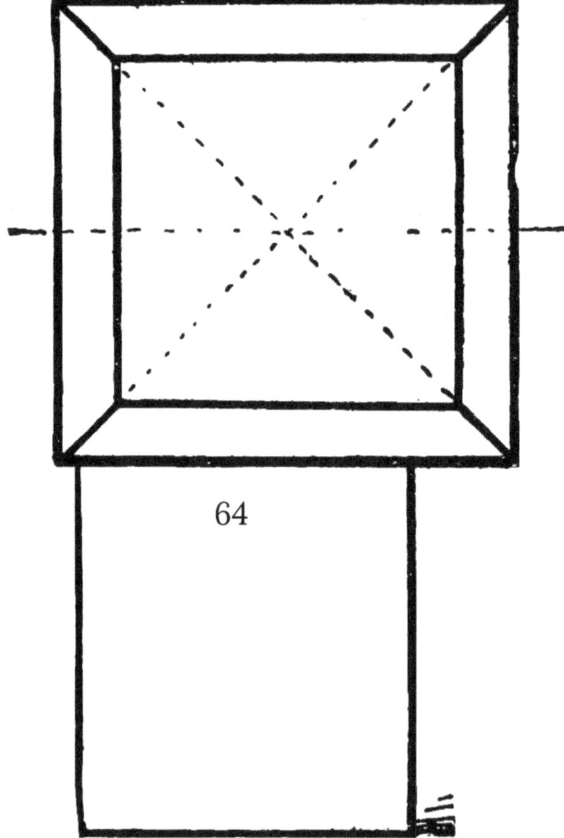

FIGURE 64. – (1) Place a cubical pasteboard box before the class so that they can see the inside.

(2) Draw it on the blackboard.

(3) Lead the class to see that all the twelve lines of the box can be seen.

(4) Minnie may take the box and hold it before her eye in the same position as the drawing on the board. Point to each line in the drawing and find its corresponding line on the box.

(5) George may take the pointer and point to the vertical parallel lines. To the horizontal

parallel lines. To the receding parallel lines. To a vertical face. To two vertical receding faces. To two horizontal receding faces.

(6) James may take the pointer and point to the center of vision. What does it represent? Point to your center of vision. Point to the horizon line. What does it represent? Where is your horizon line?

(7) Let the class draw a similar box.

(8) Drill the class at the blackboard by letting each draw a square, and then, with crayon in hand, mark a center of vision in each square and let the pupil finish the box.

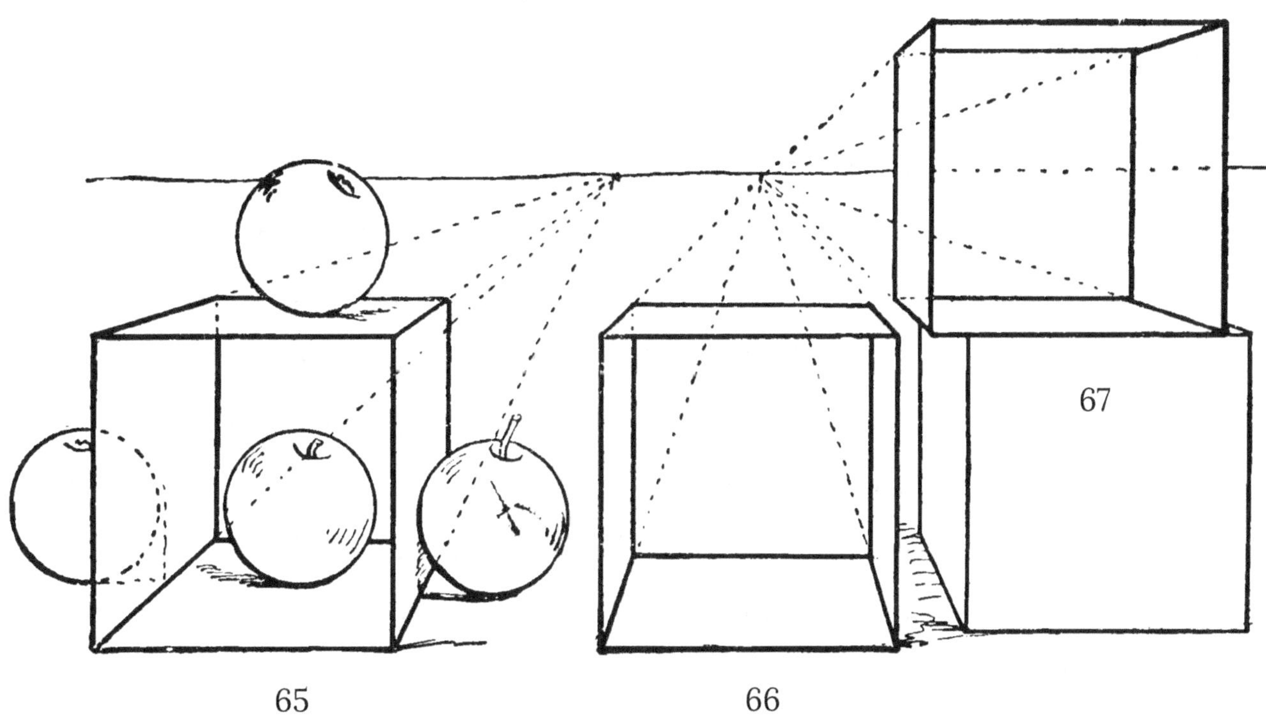

65

66

67

FIGURE 65, 66, 67. – (1) Draw boxes on the blackboard below the eye (Fig. 66), at the right of the eye (Fig. 67), and below and at the left of the eye (Fig. 65).

(2) Drill on pointing to the three classes of parallel lines.

(3) Drill on pointing to the three kinds of surfaces.

(4) Drill on holding the cube in the same position as the drawing and pointing to corresponding lines.

(5) Drill on the horizon line and center of vision.

(6) Let the class draw the box in each position.

(7) Drill the class at the blackboard by letting each draw a square and marking the center of vision somewhere about it, and letting each finish the cube.

FIGURE 67–74 – represent a common chalk box in various positions with the cover pulled partway out. When giving these lessons to the class, the box should be placed before the class in such a manner as it is drawn on the board. Of course, it is impossible for the whole class to see the box in the same position, but this is not a serious difficulty, for as soon as the principle is understood and the pupil has been sufficiently drilled in holding the box to correspond with the drawing on the blackboard, he will be able to see the box from the standpoint of the drawing with little difficulty. Each pupil should be drilled until he can do this.

A simple story associated with each drawing is very effective in stimulating and creating interest.

Review until firmly fixed in the mind the following points:

(1) Corners.

67

68

69

70

71

72

73

74

75

76

77

(2) The three kinds of lines.

(3) The three kinds of parallel lines.

(4) The three kinds of surfaces.

(5) The horizon line.

(6) The center of vision.

REVIEW BY

(1) *Questions.* — Why, how, and what?

(2) *Observation.* — Pointing to similar lines, surfaces, and principles both indoors and out.

(3) *Action.* — By acting or pointing out the various lines, surfaces, and principles.

(4) *Copying.* — By making similar drawings on the tablet or blackboard.

(5) *Problems.* — By drilling with problems illustrating some principle or truth.

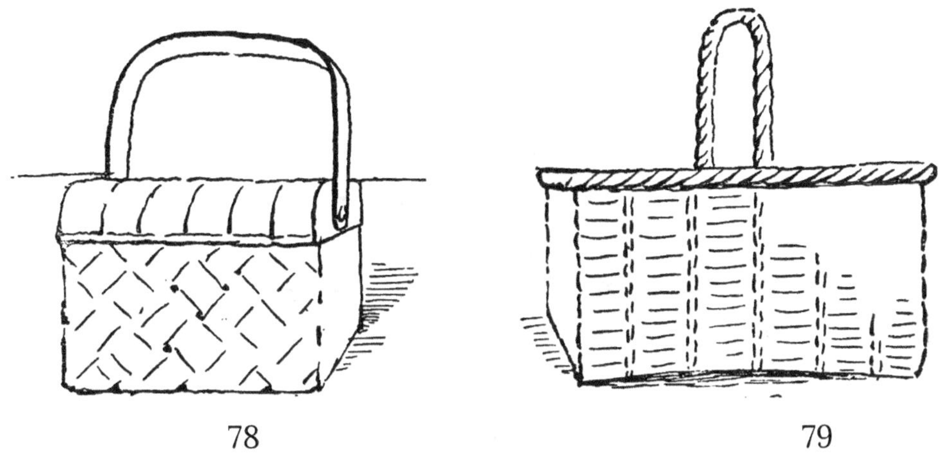

78   79

APPLICATION OF THE CUBE OR BOX TO SIMILAR FORMS.

FIGURE 78. – (1) Draw the crayon box on the blackboard at the left with the top on a level with the eye.

(2) Let the class draw a similar one.

(3) Turn the drawing into a basket.

(4) Let the class do likewise.

FIGURE 79. – (1) Draw the crayon box on the blackboard with the side toward you and a little to the right of the eye.

(2) Change it into a basket.

(3) Let the class do likewise.

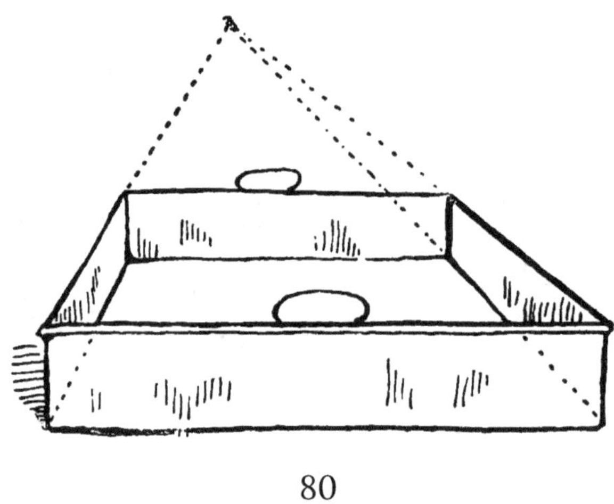

80

FIGURE 80. – (1) Take the cover of a pasteboard box and, holding it in one hand, with the other draw it on the blackboard.

(2) Change it into a frying pan.

(3) Let the class do likewise.

81

FIGURE 81. – (1) Draw a box or cube on the blackboard.

(2) Place a thatched roof on the cube.

(3) Add the door and windows.

(4) Draw a palm tree by the side of the hut with coconuts showing.

(5) Let the class do likewise.

82

FIGURE 82. – (1) Draw a crayon box on the blackboard.

(2) Add a roof to the top of the box.

(3) Finish the hut or cabin.

(4) Let the class do likewise.

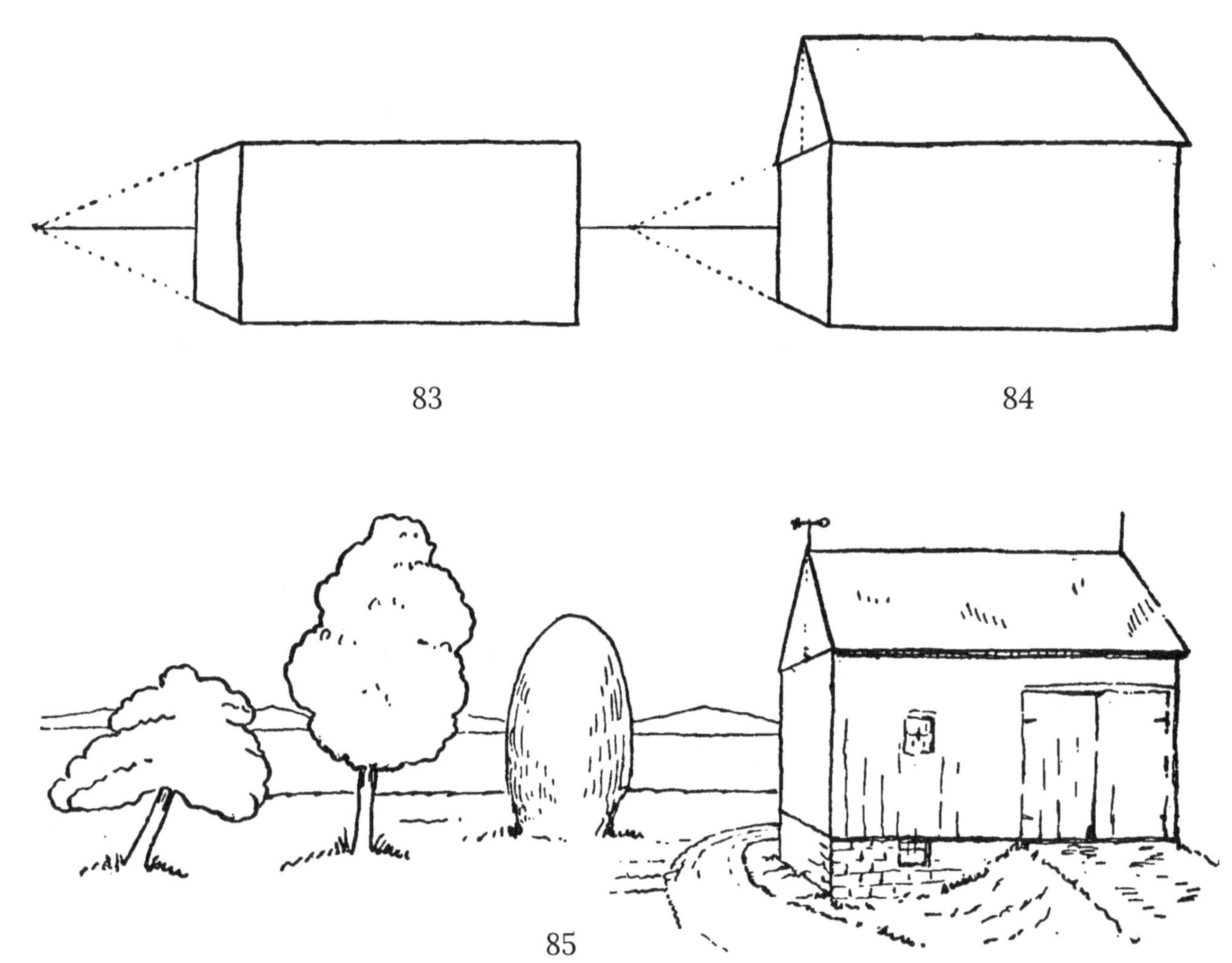

FIGURE 83 - 85. – (1) Draw a box as in Fig. 83.

(2) Place a roof on the box as in Fig. 84. Ask the class what this drawing resembles. A chorus of answers will be given, such as a barn, a house, etc. Teacher thinks it looks like a barn.

(3) What is necessary to complete our barn? Another chorus of answers; a window, a door, big doors, etc. Choose from the answers given and draw from them more definite directions. For example, a door is suggested. What kind of door? Where shall it be placed? A large door or small? Shall it be open or shut? etc. Sometimes place the object in an impossible position, such as a door in the roof, in order to give the pupils a chance to correct the drawing.

(4) After finishing the barn, ask what shall we put around our barn? Another chorus of answers. A tree, an apple tree, a haystack, etc. If objects are suggested which are difficult to draw, you may say they are behind the barn, or in the barn, etc. For example, if some pupil wants a cow or horse drawn in the road or under the trees, you can say that the horse is back of the barn. You may draw his head showing at the corner if you wish.

(5) By judicious questioning, the class may be led to suggest the entire picture the teacher has planned.

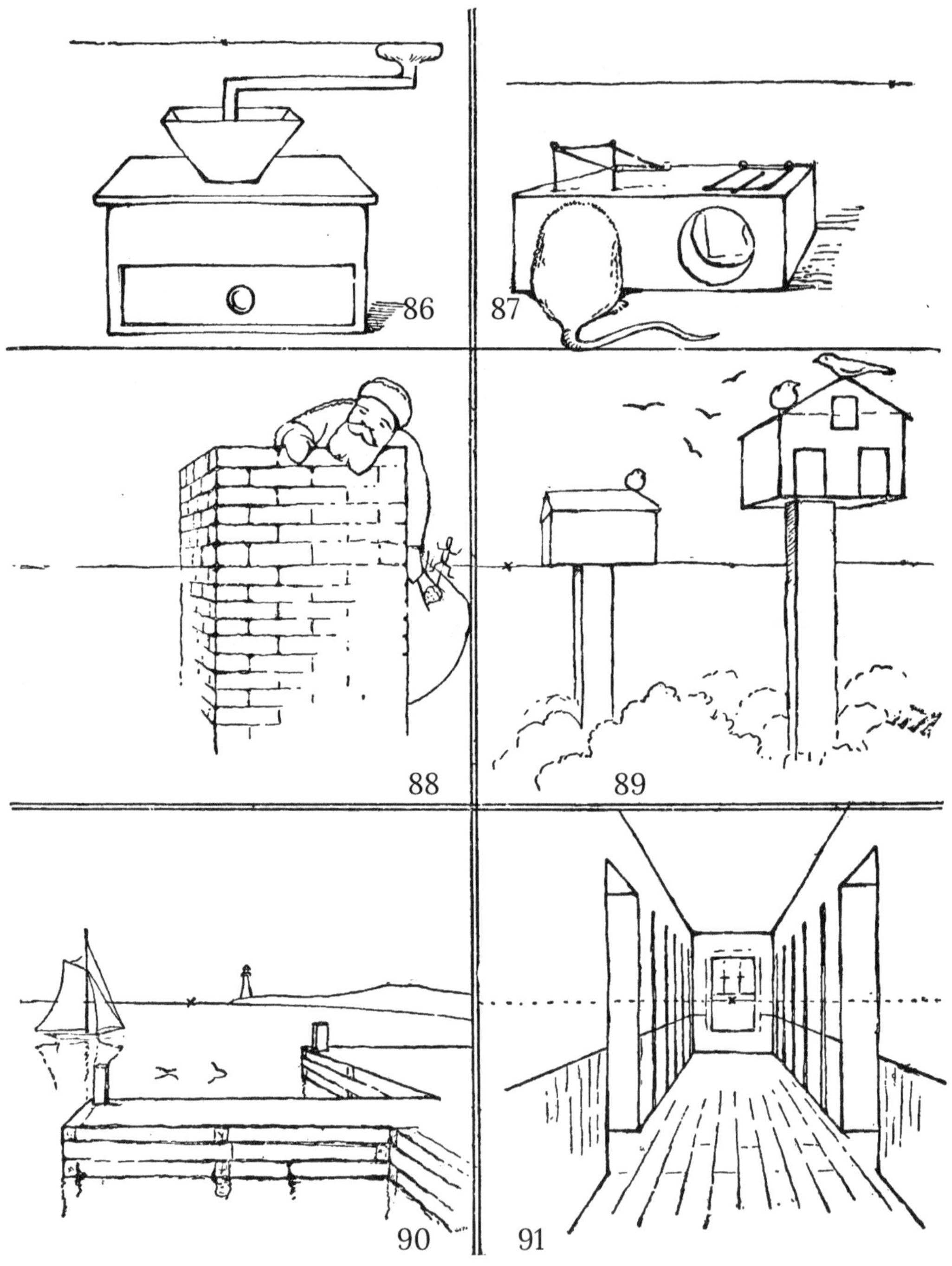

86
87
88
89
90
91

FIGURE 86 - 91. – are practical applications of the box and may be used very much as Figs. 78–85.

Fig. 86 is the same as a box below the eye. Fig. 87 is below and at the left of the eye. Fig. 88 is at the right of the eye. Fig. 89 is above and at the right of the eye. Fig. 90 is below the eye, and Fig. 91 is the interior of a box directly in front of the eye, similar to Fig. 64.

Lead the class to find objects similar to these both in the schoolroom and outdoors. Whenever a point is learned in the class, see that it is used outside of the class.

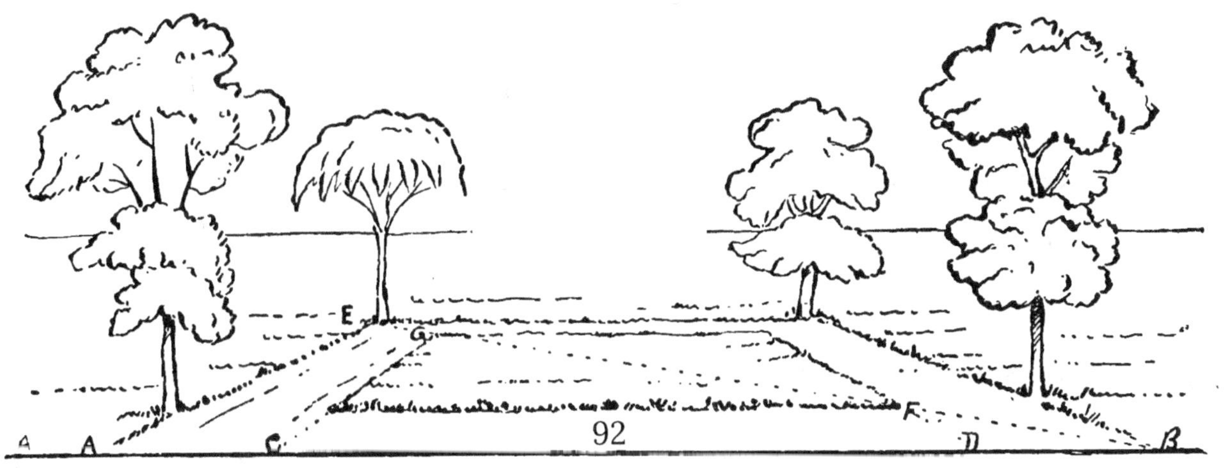

FIGURE 92. – This is an application of the top face of the cube. It represents a square plot of ground with a path around it.

Figure 92 may be drawn as follows:

(1) Draw the horizon line.

(2) Draw the line A B, the length of the plot.

(3) Choose the center of vision, also the points C and D.

(4) From the points A, B, C, and D, draw receding lines.

(5) Choose the point E and draw the diagonal line E B, which will give the points G and F.

(6) From the points E, G, and F, draw horizontal lines, finishing the square plot and the path around it.

Let several pupils compare the plot with the top face of the cube. The trees on the left are elm trees. The first one on the right is a chestnut and the further one is an oak.

RECAPITULATION.

Before proceeding to the cylinder, a pupil should be able to draw the box:

(1) Below, above, and in front of the eye.

(2) At the right and left of the eye.

(3) Above and at the right and left of the eye.

(4) Below and at the right and left of the eye.

(5) To remove the top, side, bottom, and front faces in each position.

(6) To be able to hold the box in the hand in the same position as the drawing and to point to corresponding lines in each.

The child should also be able to recognize both on the object and in the drawing:

(1) The three kinds of lines.

(2) The three kinds of parallel lines.

(3) The three kinds of surfaces.

(4) To know the horizon line and center of vision.

PART III.

THE CYLINDER.

The study of the cylinder is divided into:

(1) The vertical cylinder.

(2) The horizontal cylinder.

(3) The receding cylinder.

A common fruit can is a very good model. Several of them, of various sizes, should be procured and used often. Remove the end from one or two of the cans so as to show a hollow cylinder.

Each pupil should be required to make a cylinder for himself. This may be done from cardboard, clay, plaster of Paris, or whittled from wood.

THE VERTICAL CYLINDER.

Begin drawing the cylinder at once without explaining any part until the pupils have become familiar with the outline in one position. They will become familiar with it by drawing and seeing you draw it sooner than in any other way.

This one position should be the position most commonly seen by the pupil, such as those represented by Figs. 1 - 16.

The general plan is as follows: (1) Place the cylinder before the class in the position to be drawn, as in Figs. 1 - 16. (2) Draw this position on the blackboard and let the pupils draw a similar one on their tablets. (3) Introduce some device that will interest the class and stimulate a desire to draw the picture. A story connected with the drawing is very effective in doing this. (4) Drill with the class at the blackboard.

FIGURE 3 – 10 are devices that may be introduced with the cylinder in the classroom before the pupils.

FIGURE 11 – 16 are devices appealing to the memory and imagination.

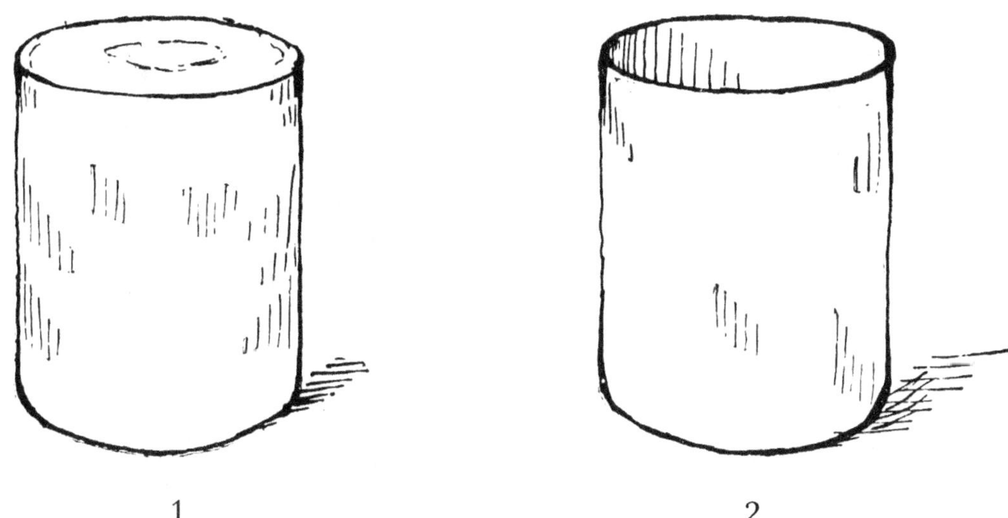

1   2

FIGURE 1. – (1) Place the cylinder before the class.

(2) Draw it on the blackboard.

(3) Let the class draw a similar cylinder.

(4) Draw a cylinder in a conspicuous place on the blackboard and let it remain until the next lesson, as a silent teacher.

FIGURE 2. – (1) Use a cylinder with one end removed.

(2) Place it before the class so that the solid end shows.

(3) Draw it on the blackboard.

(4) Let the class draw a similar cylinder.

(5) Turn the cylinder showing the end removed. Represent the end as removed in the drawing.

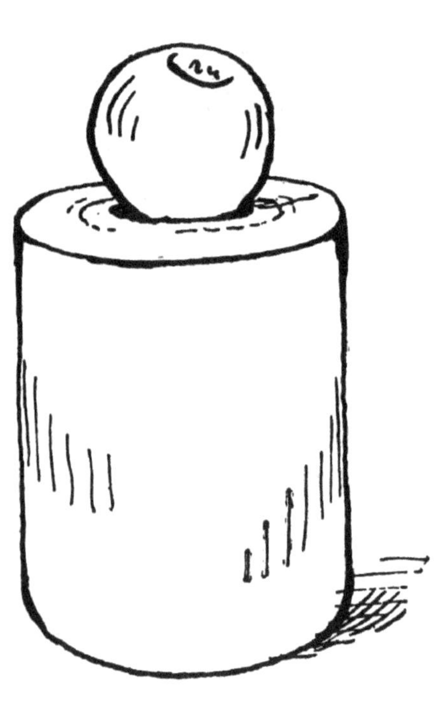

3

4

FIGURE 3. – (1) Place the cylinder before the class, draw it on the board, and let the class make a similar drawing.

(2) Place an apple on the cylinder, represent it in the drawing, and let the pupils do likewise.

In like manner, draw Figs. 4 - 10 and let the class draw similar ones. Draw only one cylinder with its accessories for a lesson. Review the work by drilling at the board thus:

(1) Send the class to the board and let each draw a cylinder.

(2) Let one draw an apple resting on top of his cylinder; another a pear; another a lemon, etc. Let each one remove the top from his cylinder and fill it with cherries, tomatoes, plums, etc.

5

6

7

8

9

10

SURFACES.

TEACH A

(1) Plane face or surface.

(2) Curved face or surface.

(3) Round face or surface.

A *plane face* is a flat surface like the ends of the cylinder or the faces of a cube.

A *curved surface* curves in one direction like the side of a cylinder.

A *round surface* curves in all directions like the surface of a sphere.

Use a cylinder and cube to teach the plane face; a cylinder to teach the curved face; and the sphere to teach the round face.

A plane face or surface may be vertical, vertically receding, or horizontally receding, and may be taught in the same manner as the different kinds of lines were taught.

A curved face may be vertical, horizontal, or receding, corresponding to the three positions of the cylinder.

11

FIGURE 11. – (1) Draw a cylinder and a sphere on the board.

(2) Take a cylinder and a sphere in the hand and show a plane, a curved, and a round surface.

(3) Charles may take the cylinder and point to a plane face; a curved face; to two plane faces; ask if the cylinder has more than one curved face. Point to a curved surface in the drawing on the board; a plane surface; find a plane surface in the room; a curved surface; a round surface. Represent a round, a curved, and a plane surface on the blackboard.

(4) Draw a kingfisher perched on the cylinder with a worm in its mouth.

(5) Tell the story of the boy who went fishing with his bait in a fruit can, and how he left his bait on the bank of the stream while fishing. Explain how another fisherman (a kingfisher) came along and, by means of its long bill, ate all the worms which were used for bait. When

the boy went to get more worms to put on his hook, none could be found, and he was puzzled to know what had become of them.

(6) Hold a box in the hand and show that a plane may be vertical, vertically receding, or horizontally receding.

FIGURE 12. – (1) Draw the cylinder on the blackboard.

(2) Hold a cylinder in the hand.

(3) Mary, how many faces has the cylinder? How many plane faces? Curved surfaces? Take the cylinder and point to each surface, naming it as you point.

(4) John, how many edges has the cylinder? Point to them. Are the edges straight or curved? Has the cylinder corners?

(5) Minnie, take the pointer and point to a plane face in the drawing on the blackboard; to a curved face; to the line that represents the edges.

(6) Represent the picture of an ear of corn on the can, and print "sweet corn" on the side.

(7) Draw a long-legged bird with its head and neck in the can.

(8) Tell the story of how Bridget placed a can of sweet corn at the door to cool and how a long-legged bird came along and helped himself without asking leave.

13

FIGURE 13. – (1) Place the cylinder before the class, draw it on the blackboard, and let the class draw a similar one.

(2) Tell the story of a little girl who filled a fruit can part full of dirt, planted some flower seeds in it, and placed the can in a warm place outdoors. She forgot about the seeds and left them unattended. One day, she remembered them and went to check, only to find a nest built in the top of the can with an old mother bird sitting patiently on it.

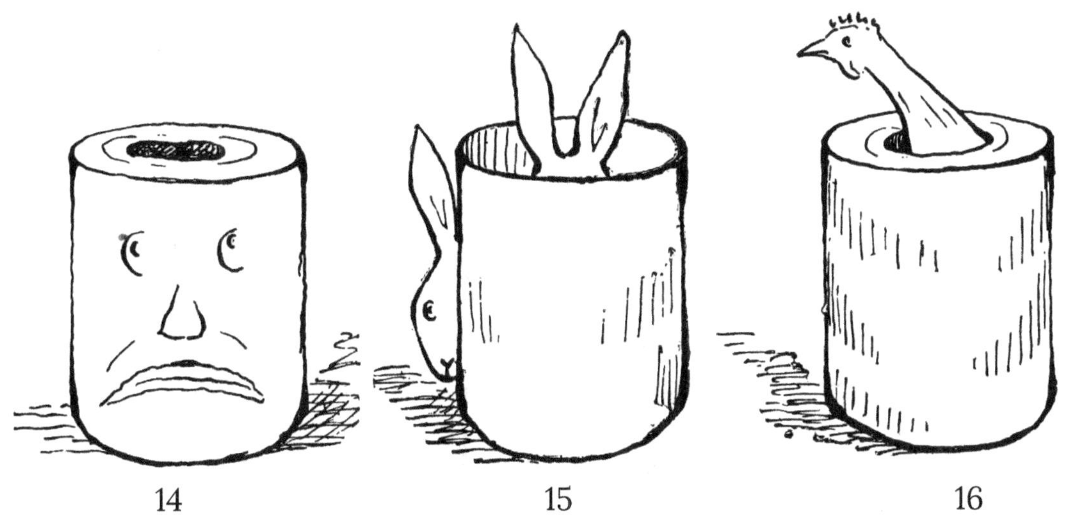

14   15   16

FIGURE 14. – (1) Place a cylinder before the class, draw it on the blackboard, and let the class draw a similar one.

(2) Tell the story of how a mischievous boy procured some paint and painted a hideous face on a fruit can to frighten his little sisters.

FIGURE 15. – (1) Place the cylinder before the class. Draw it on the blackboard, and let the pupils draw a similar one.

(2) Tell the story of two rabbits that were chased by dogs. One hid in a fruit can, and the other got behind it to hide from the dogs. Keep up the practice of drawing and drilling from the cylinder in one position until the pupils can draw it in this position fairly well. Do not lay the model aside but use it continually. Let the class see that it is the source of the drawing. When the proper time comes for drawing from the real cylinder, the pupils can do so with little trouble.

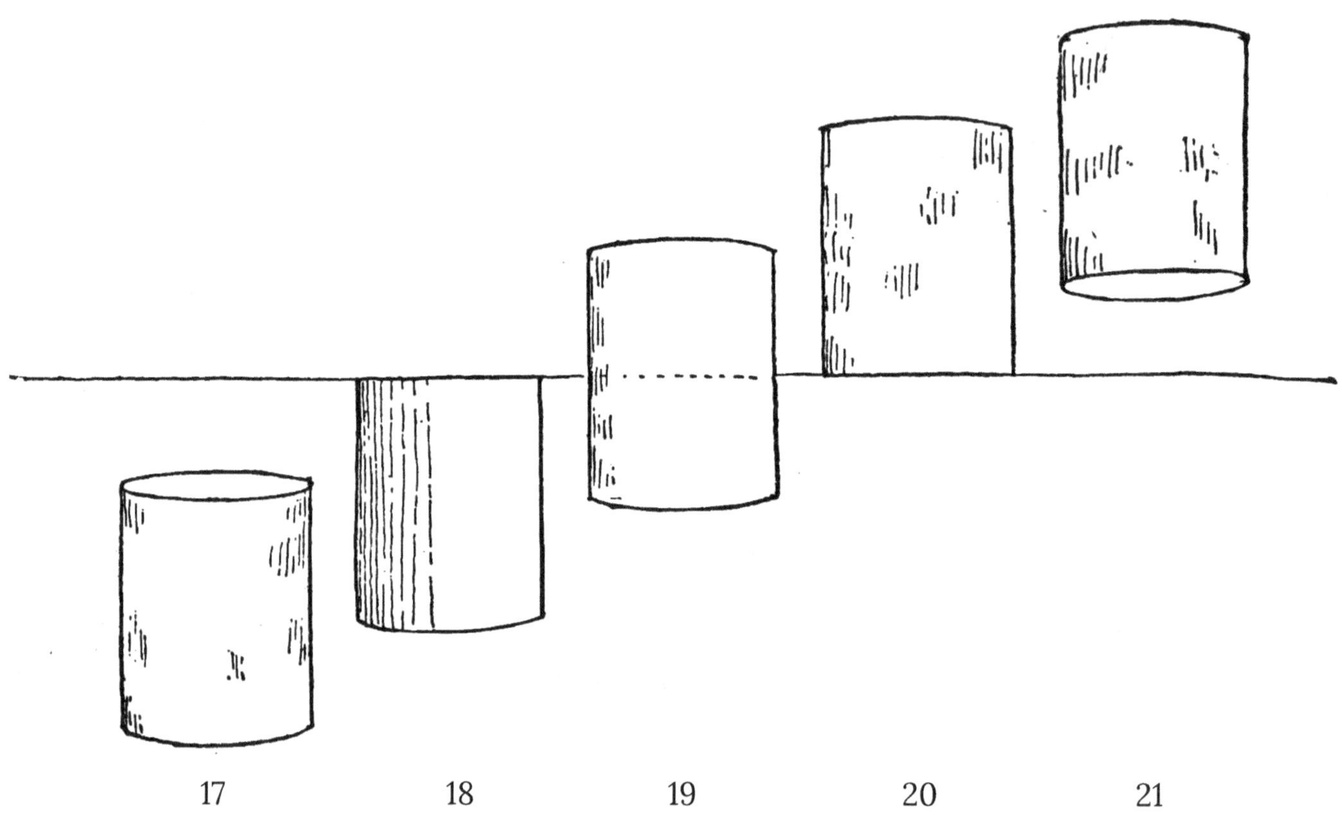

17   18   19   20   21

FIGURE 17 - 21. – (1) Review the level of the eye.

(2) Peter may take the pointer and hold it horizontally above the eye, below the eye, and on a level with the eye.

(3) Place objects in various parts of the room and ask if they are above the eye, below the eye, or on a level with the eye.

(4) Hold a cylinder vertically before the class and below the level of their eyes. Ask, can you see the top face? Can you see the bottom face?

(5) Hold the cylinder in the same manner above the eye, and ask if they can see the bottom, if they can see the top.

(6) Hold the cylinder about on a level with their eyes and ask if they can see either the top or the bottom.

APPLICATIONS OF THE VERTICAL CYLINDER.

What is like a vertical cylinder? Encourage each pupil to find many objects as he can that resemble the vertical cylinder. Encourage this work in the following manner: Draw a cylinder on the blackboard and change it into forms that are like a cylinder. The child knows the type form, and when it is turned into a similar form he sees the resemblance at once and will connect the two whenever seen afterward.

FIGURE 22 - 24. – (1) Draw a cylinder above, below, and on a level with the eye, and turn each into a cheese box.

(2) Pupils may make a similar drawing.

(3) Charles, why can you see the bottom of the upper box? Why cannot the top be seen? Why is the curved line that marks the top of the box in Fig. 23 a horizontal line? Why can the top of Fig. 24 be seen? In Fig. 24, which line will curve more, the one that marks the top, or the one that marks the bottom?

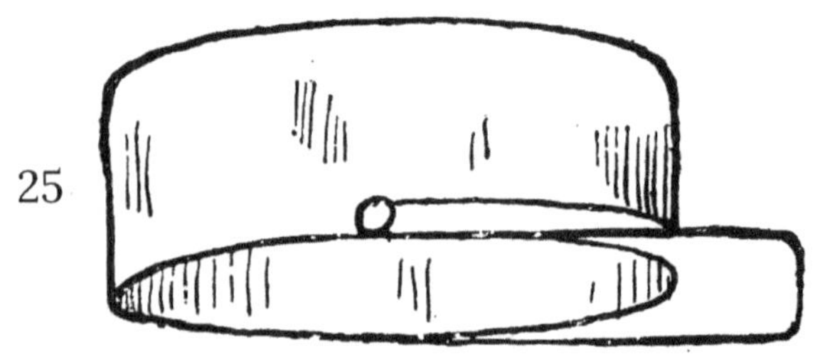

25

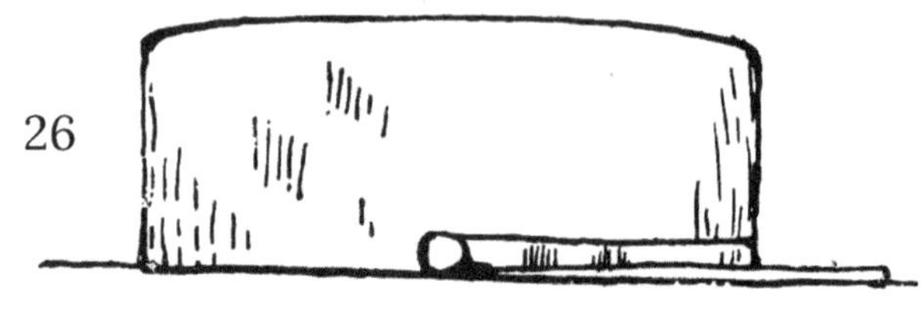

26

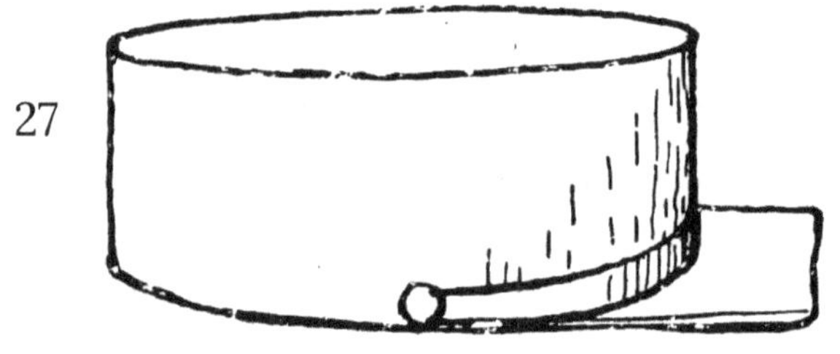

27

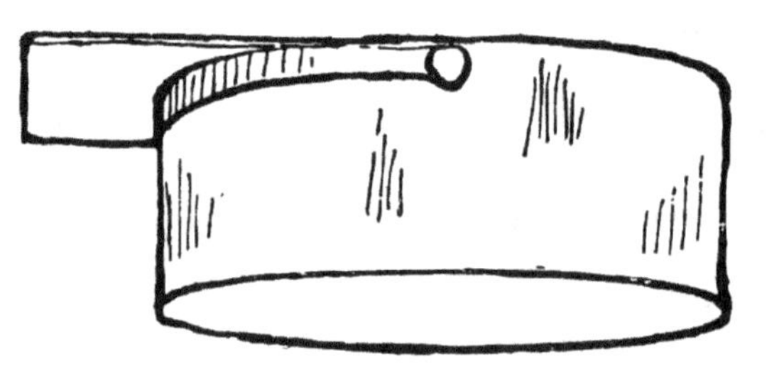

28

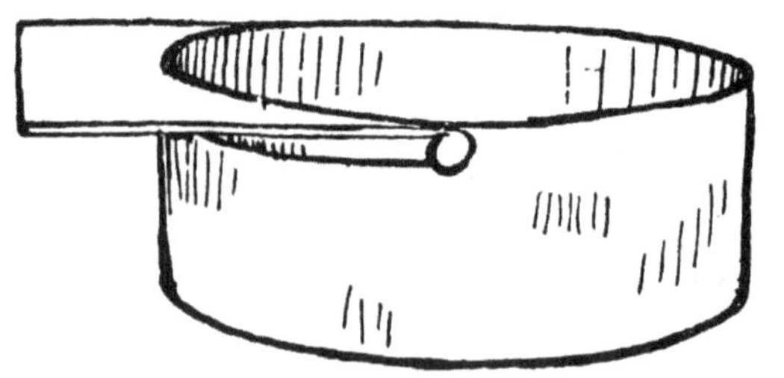

29

30

FIGURE 25 - 30. – (1) Draw a cylinder in each of these positions and turn them into caps.

(2) James may take a cap and hold it in the position of Fig. 25, Fig. 26, Fig. 27, Fig. 28, Fig. 29, Fig. 30.

(3) Drill at the blackboard as follows: John may draw a cylinder above the level of the eye and turn it into a cap with the open part downward. Mary may do the same with the cylinder below the eye. Minnie may do the same with the bottom of the cylinder on a level with the eye.

(4) Let each member of the class draw a cylinder on the blackboard and turn it into Fig. 28, Fig. 30, Fig. 25, Fig. 27.

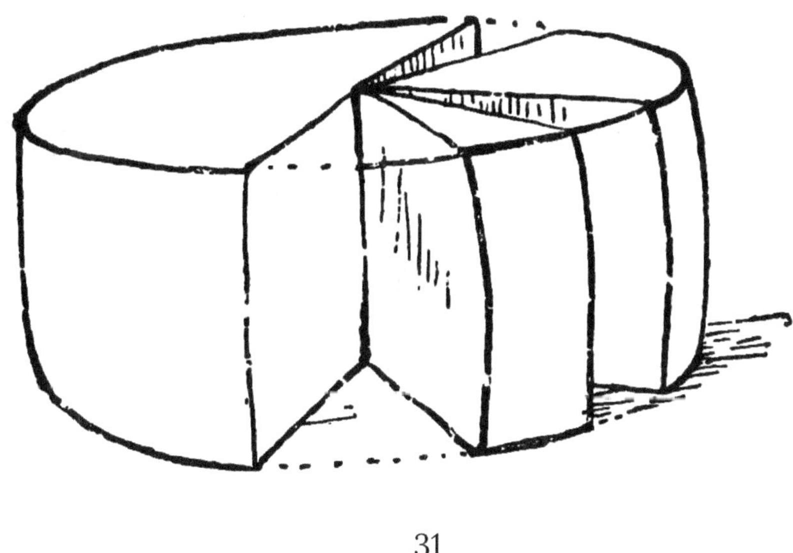

31

FIGURE 31. – (1) Draw a cylinder on the blackboard and let the pupils draw a similar one.

(2) Cut slices out of the cylinder after the manner of slices from a cheese.

(3) Drill with easy problems at the blackboard.

32

FIGURE 32. – (1) Draw a cylinder below the level of the eye on the blackboard and let the pupils draw a similar one.

(2) Turn it into a stump.

(3) Represent the stump as hollow.

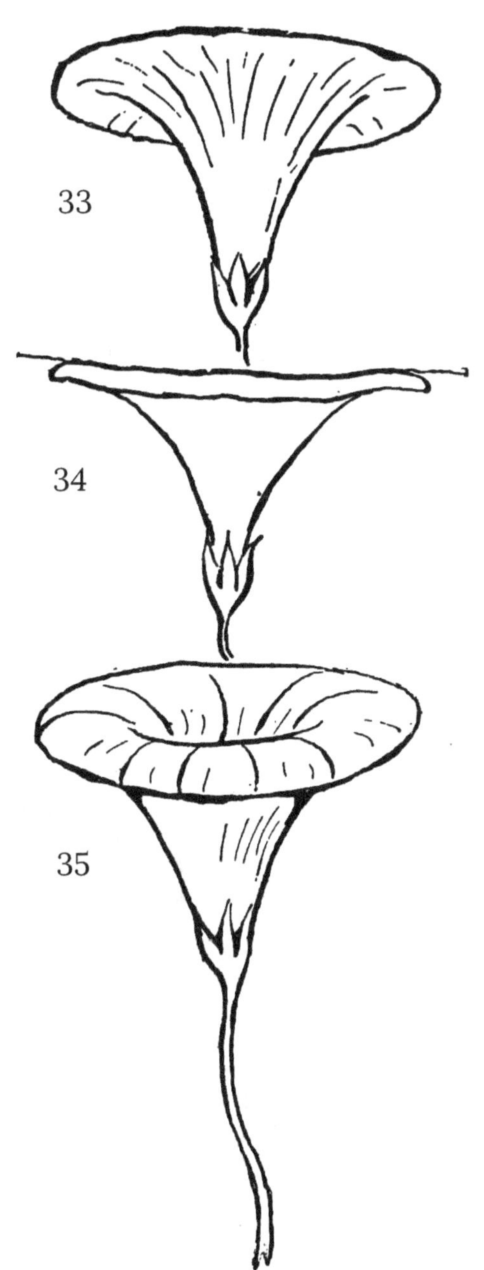

33

34

35

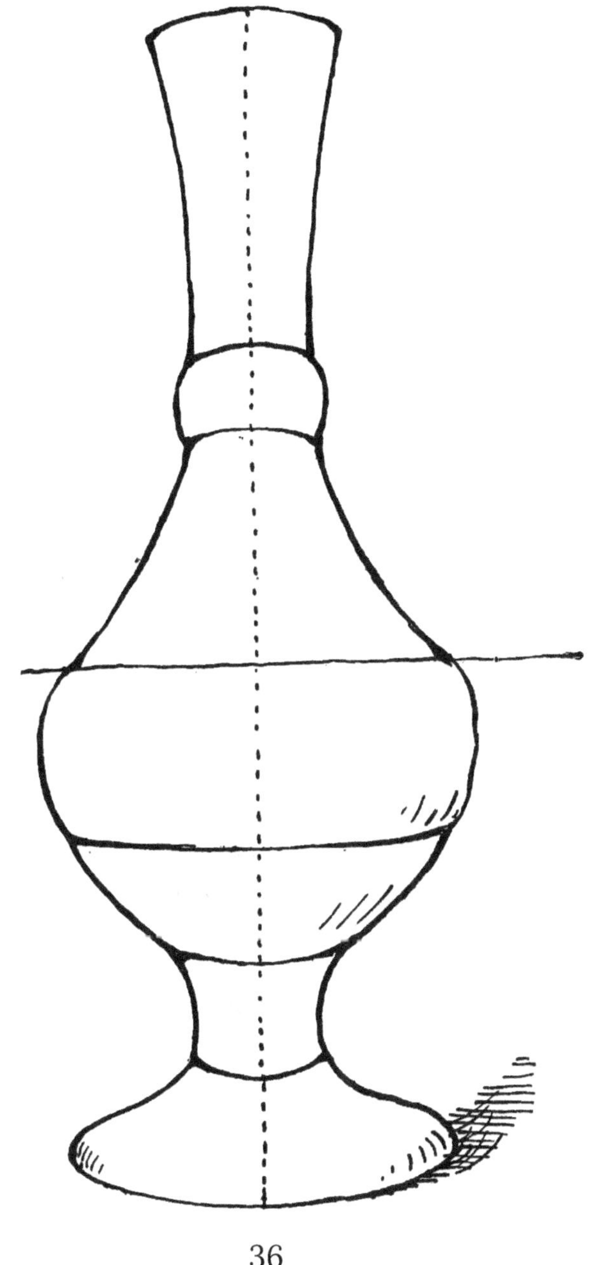

36

FIGURE 33 - 35. – (1) Represent a flower based on a vertical cylinder drawn above, below, and on a level with the eye.

(2) Draw them on the blackboard and let the class draw similar ones.

(3) Drill the class at the blackboard.

FIGURE 36. – (1) Draw a vase on the blackboard with the middle on a level with the eye, and let the class draw a similar one.

(2) Peter, take the pointer and point to the level of the eye. Why do the lines below that line curve downward? Why do the lines above that line curve upward? Why cannot you see into the vase? Can you place the horizon line in such a position that you could see into the vase?

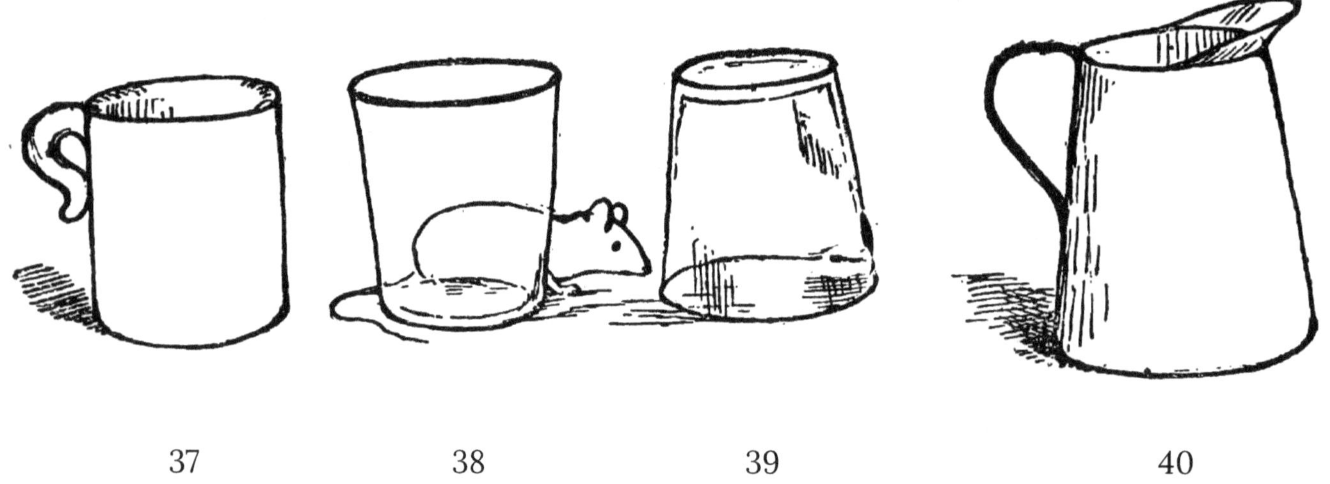

37   38   39   40

41

42

43

44

45

46

FIGURE 37. – (1) Draw a cylinder on the blackboard and turn it into a mug.

(2) Let the pupils draw a similar one.

(3) Drill as follows at the blackboard: Draw a mug below the eye. With the rim on a level with the eye. With the middle part of the mug on a level with the eye. With the bottom part of the mug on a level with the eye.

FIGURE 38 - 46. – are simple applications of the vertical cylinder; they may be drawn as follows:

(1) Draw a cylinder on the blackboard about the same proportions as the object into which it is to be turned.

(2) Turn the cylinder into the object.

(3) Add the accessories with an appropriate story or device to make it interesting.

(4) Drill on the position of the cylinder in regard to the eye.

(5) Let the pupils reproduce the drawings on the blackboard from memory.

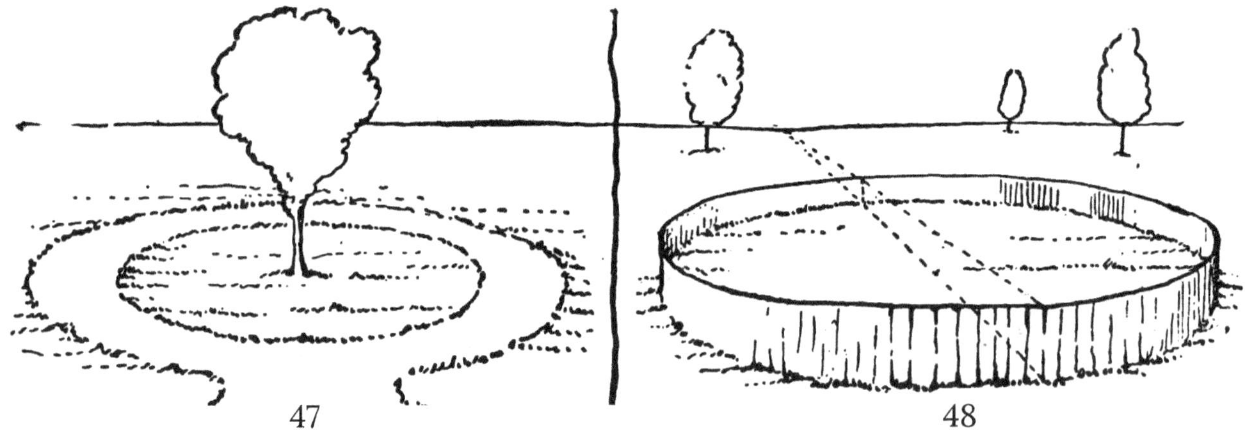

47   48

49

50

51

52

53

54

FIGURE 47 - 54. – are applications of the vertical cylinder that are not so apparent as the others.

Figure 47 represents the ends of two cylinders, one within the other, and below the level of the eye.

Figure 48 is a very shallow cylinder with the top removed.

Figure 47is on the level ground, Fig. 48 is built up from the ground, and Fig. 49 is sunk below the surface of the ground.

Figure 50 represents a circular pond with reflections in it.

FIGURE 51. – represents a round island with reflections.

FIGURE 52. – represents the Monitor with its cylindrical turret and funnel, with the Merrimac in the distance.

FIGURE 53. – is a tower with the top above the level of the eye, and a low of trees extending to the horizon line.

FIGURE 54. – represents stumps at various levels, showing how they appear above and below the level of the eye.

The following are a number of simple problems that may be drawn from Figs. 47 – 54 and used for drill, and to give variety to the work.

(1) Draw a square plat of ground similar to Fig. 47 and place a tree in the center.

(2) Sink the center of Fig. 47 so low in the ground as not to show the bottom.

(3) Raise the center of Fig. 47 above the level of the ground, until it is on a level with the eye.

(4) Sink Fig. 48 as low in the ground as the top of the fence is above the ground.

(5) Represent Fig. 48 with the top of the fence on a level with the eye.

(6) Elevate the center of Fig. 49 as high above the ground as the surface of the water is be-low the ground.

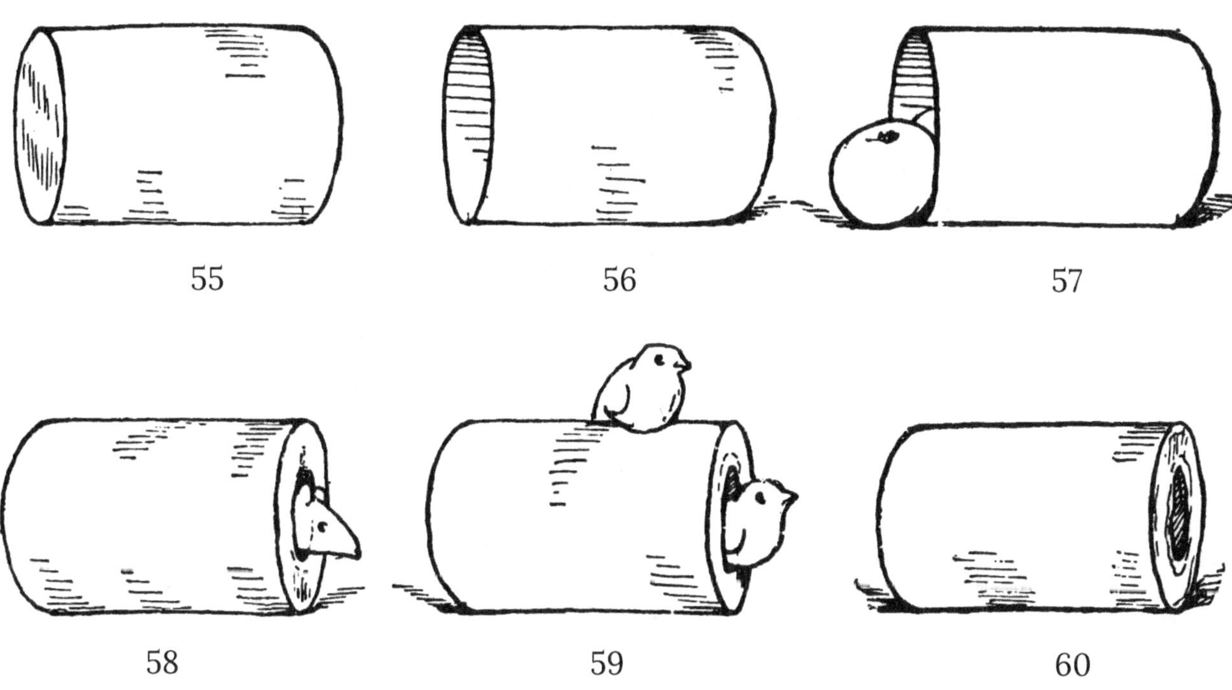

55

56

57

58

59

60

THE HORIZONTAL CYLINDER.

Place a horizontal cylinder before the class after the manner of the vertical cylinder, and draw it a number of times in the same position, first at the right of the eye as in Figs. 55 - 57, and then at the left of the eye, as in Figs. 58-60.

Associate in each lesson familiar forms, such as apples, pears, potatoes, etc., together with stories to make the work interesting and excite a desire to draw the cylinder.

61   62   63

FIGURE 61 - 63. – (1) Hold the cylinder horizontally before the class and lead them to see that when the cylinder is directly in front of the eye, the ends cannot be seen as in Fig. 62. That when the cylinder is at the right of the eye, one end will show as in Fig. 63, and when it is at the left of the eye, the other end will show as in Fig. 61.

(2) Georgia may take the cylinder and hold it in a horizontal position directly in front of the eye. Can you see either end? Hold it at the right of the eye. Can you see one end now? Hold it at the left of the eye. Can you see the same end as before?

(3) Draw a horizon line on the blackboard and in it mark a center of vision.

(4) Emphasize the fact that the center of vision is the point directly opposite the eye, and that the point you have placed on the board represents that point.

(5) Hold the cylinder against the blackboard as in Fig. 62, and ask if either end of the cylinder can be seen if drawn in this position. Draw the cylinder in this position.

(6) Hold the cylinder at the left, and at the right, and draw it. Lead the class in this way to see that when the cylinder is at the left of the center of vision, or the eye, one end can be seen, and when it is at the right, the other end can be seen. Show that when one end is even with the center of vision, or eye, that it is represented by a vertical line.

(7) Let the class draw cylinders at the left of the eye, in front of the eye, and at the right of the eye.

(8) Drill at the blackboard. All may draw a horizontal cylinder at the right of the eye; at the left of the eye; in front of the eye with one end directly in front of the eye.

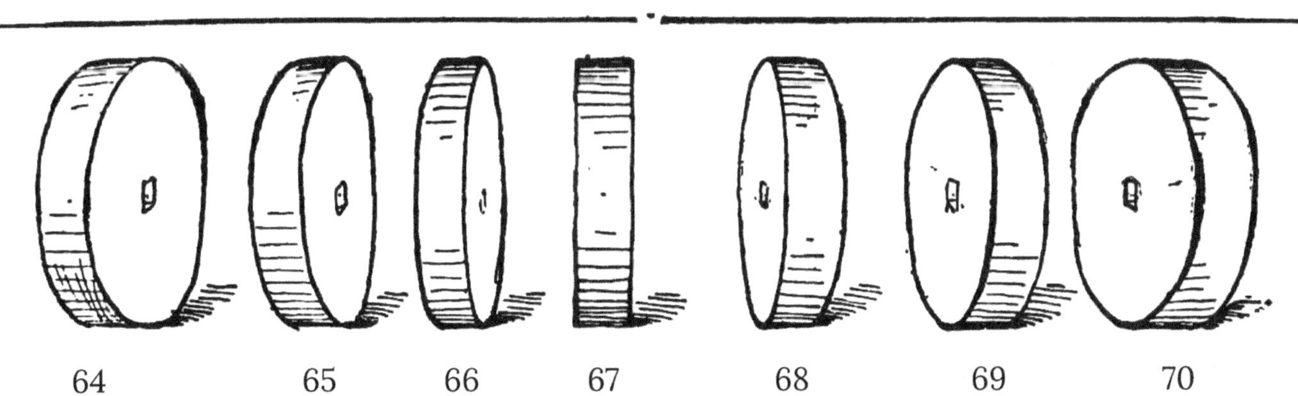

64   65   66   67   68   69   70

FIGURE 64 - 70. – (1) Draw a horizon line and in it mark a center of vision. Ask what each represents.

(2) Draw a grindstone directly below and in front of the eye, and three grindstones to the right, and three to the left of the eye.

(3) Lead the pupils to see that the further to the right or left of the eye the grindstones are, the more circular they become.

(4) Explain this more fully with the cylinder by holding it in the hand and passing it from in front of the pupil's eye to either side.

(5) Drill with the class at the board. Draw a grindstone below the eye; below and at the left; below and at the right; at the right; at the left; directly in front of the eye, etc.

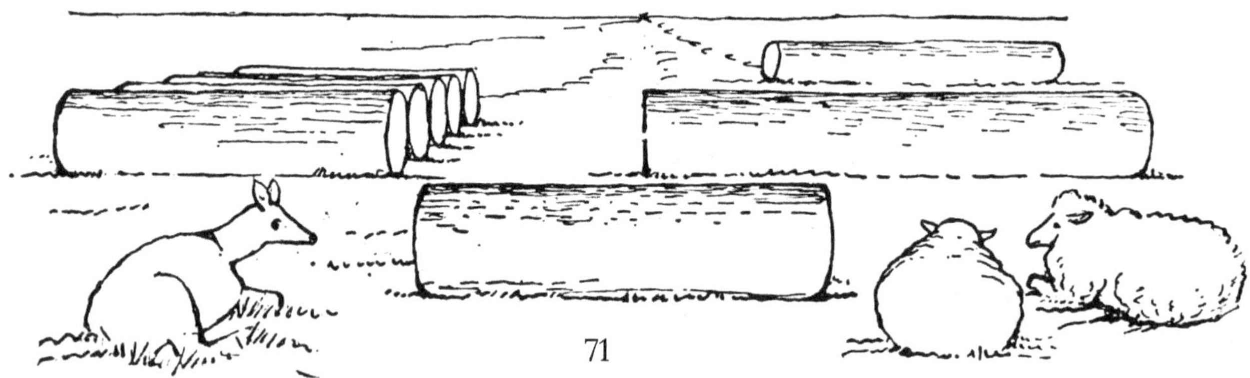

71

FIGURE 71. – (1) Draw a horizon line and in it mark a center of vision.

(2) Ask what each represents.

(3) Draw the upper and lower line of the nearest log; tell the pupils what it is to represent, and ask how to draw the ends, and why?

(4) Draw each log in the same manner and ask questions similar to the following: Which end will show? Why? How shall I draw this end? Why? etc.

(5) Let the class draw similar logs.

(6) Drill with the class at the board. Draw a log directly below the eye; below the eye with one end even with the center of vision; below and at the left and right of the eye.

(7) The animals in the drawing are to add interest to the picture.

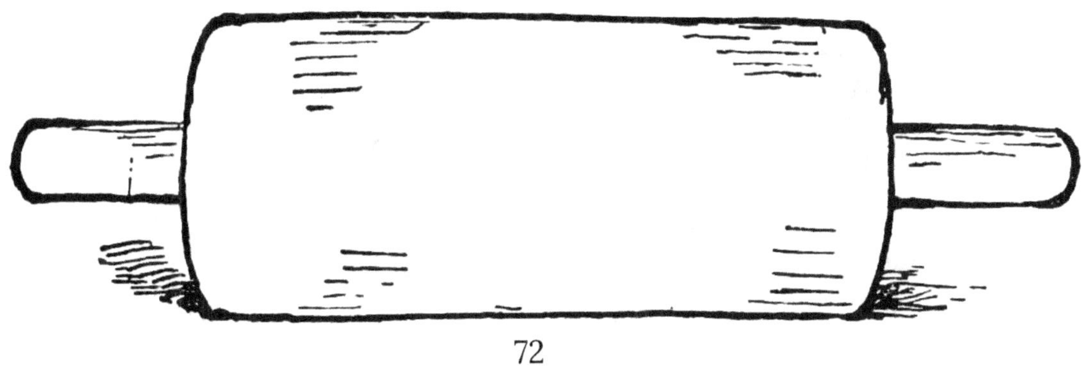

72

APPLICATIONS OF THE HORIZONTAL CYLINDER.

Lead the pupils to make a list of objects similar to the horizontal cylinder. [See page 139.]

Point out to them in nature objects that are based on this form, and get them to tell you of similar applications.

Draw cylinders on the blackboard and change them into forms that resemble the cylinder, such as Figs. 72 - 80. This is, by far, the most effective way of teaching the applications of type forms.

FIGURE 72. – (1) Draw the cylinder on the blackboard.

(2) Turn it into a rolling pin.

(3) Let the class make a similar drawing.

(4) Draw the rolling pin at the right of the eye. At the left of the eye.

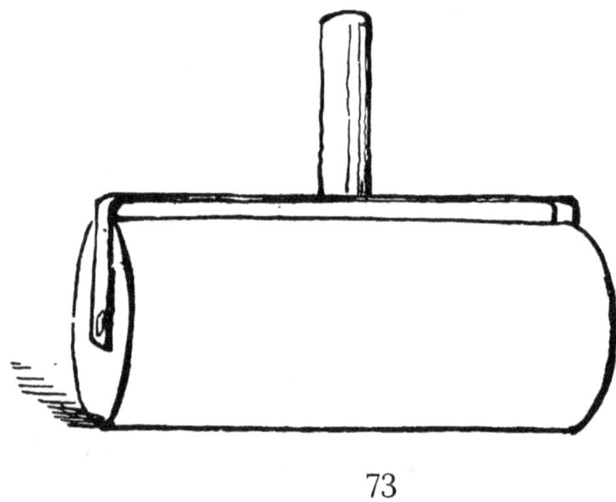

73

FIGURE 73. – (1) Draw the cylinder on the blackboard at the right of the eye.

(2) Turn it into a roller.

(3) Let the class make a similar one.

(4) Draw the roller at the left of the eye.

In like manner, draw Figs. 74 - 80, drawing each object in several positions in regard to the eye, and leading the class to do the same.

It is better to draw the same object in several positions than to draw the same number of different objects.

Draw Fig. 74 at the right of the eye.

Draw Fig. 75 at the right of the eye.

Draw Fig. 76 at the right of the eye.

Draw Fig. 77 at the left of the eye.

Draw Fig. 78 at the right of the eye, and Fig. 80 at the left of the eye.

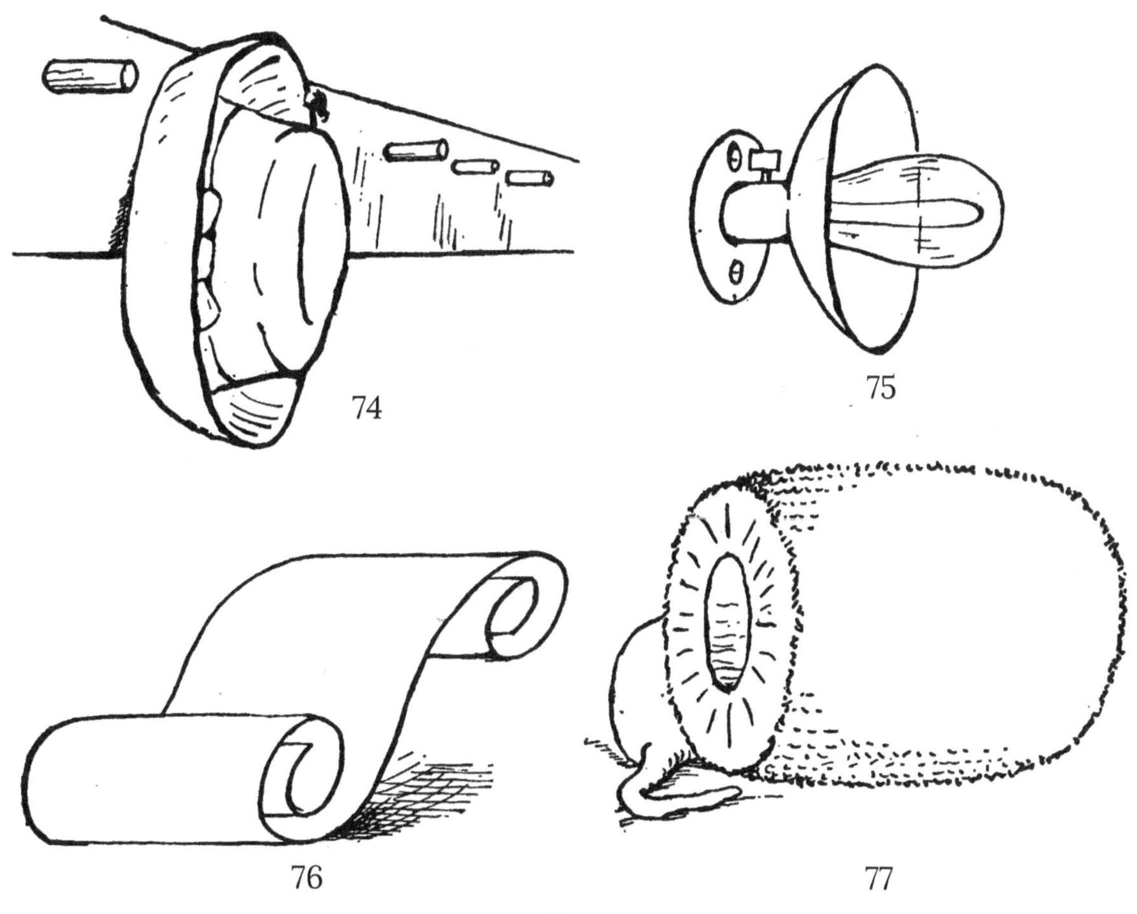

74

75

76

77

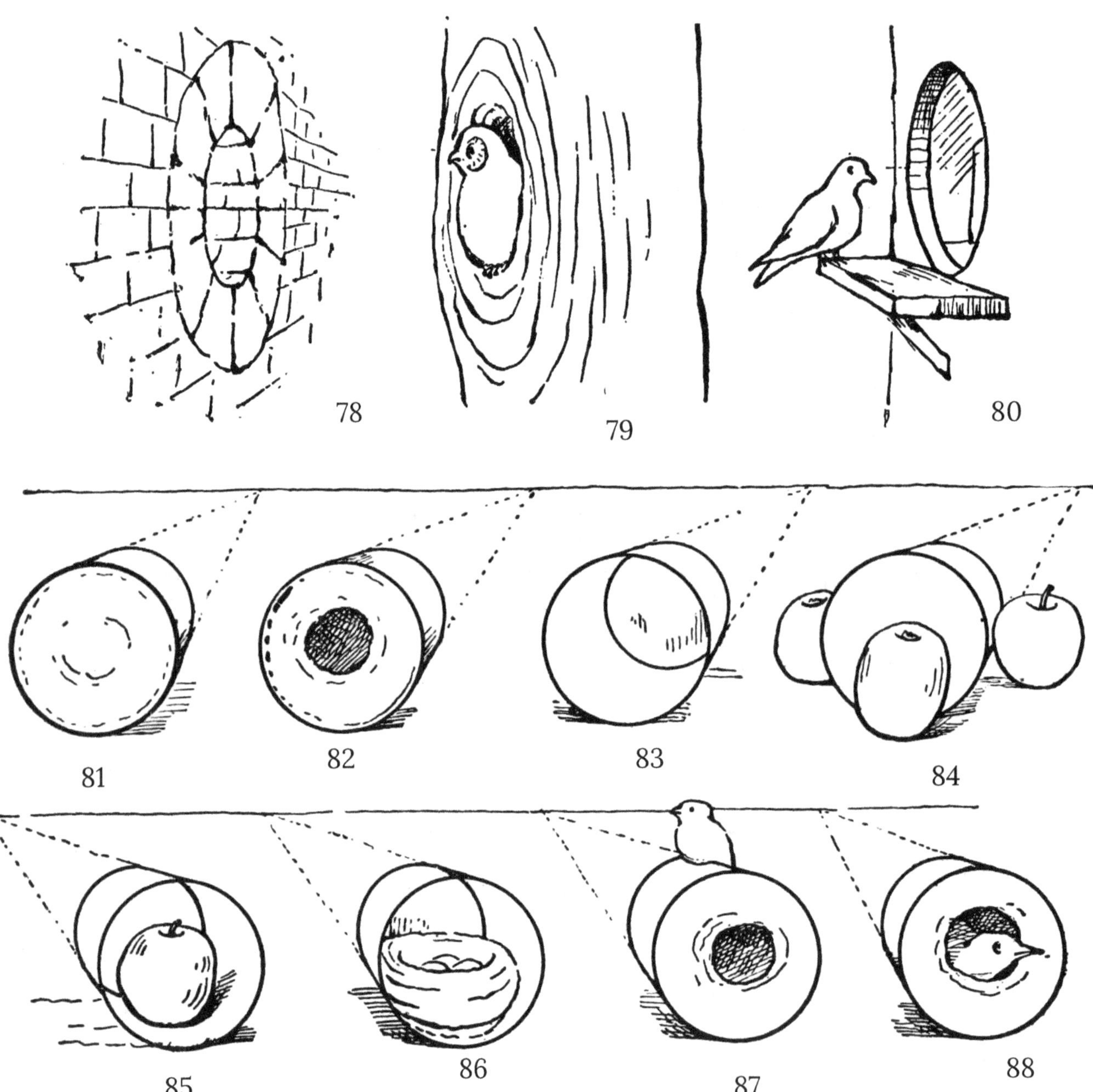

78

79

80

81

82

83

84

85

86

87

88

THE RECEDING CYLINDER.

Place a receding cylinder before the class as in Fig. 81, and draw it a number of times in the same position as in Figs. 81 - 84. Also as in figures 85 - 88.

Associate in each lesson familiar forms, such as pears, lemons, apples, birds, etc., together with stories to make the work interesting, and excite a desire to draw the cylinder.

After they have become familiar with the cylinder in one position, drill on the position of the cylinder in regard to the eye.

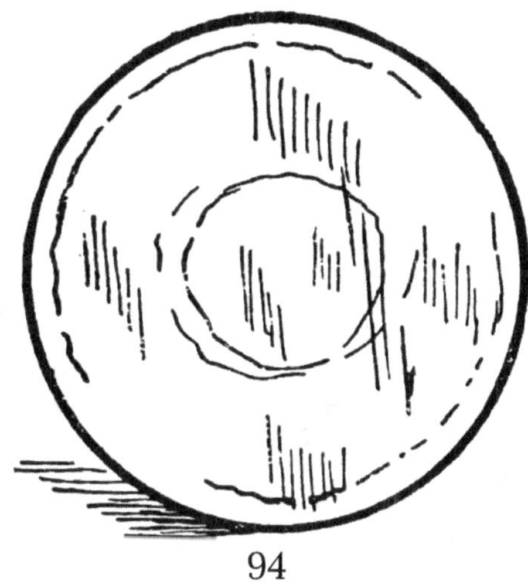

94

FIGURE 94. – (1) Hold a receding cylinder before the class in such a manner that the sides cannot be seen.

(2) What is the shape of the end? Mollie, you may choose a figure from the box shaped like the end of the cylinder.

(3) John may draw the figure on the blackboard.

FIGURE 89 – 93. – (1) Hold the cylinder in a receding position above the level of the eye. Can you see the side? Hold the cylinder below the level of the eye. Can you see the side? Hold the cylinder at the right and left of the eye. What is the shape of the end?

(2) Lead the class to see that the end is a circle in each position, that the cylinder is composed of curved and receding lines, and that part of the side can be seen.

(3) Blanche may take a cylinder. Hold it directly in front of the eye. Can you see the side? What is the shape of the end?

(4) Hold the cylinder at the right of the eye, at the left of the eye, below the eye, above the eye. Can you see the side? Is the end a circle?

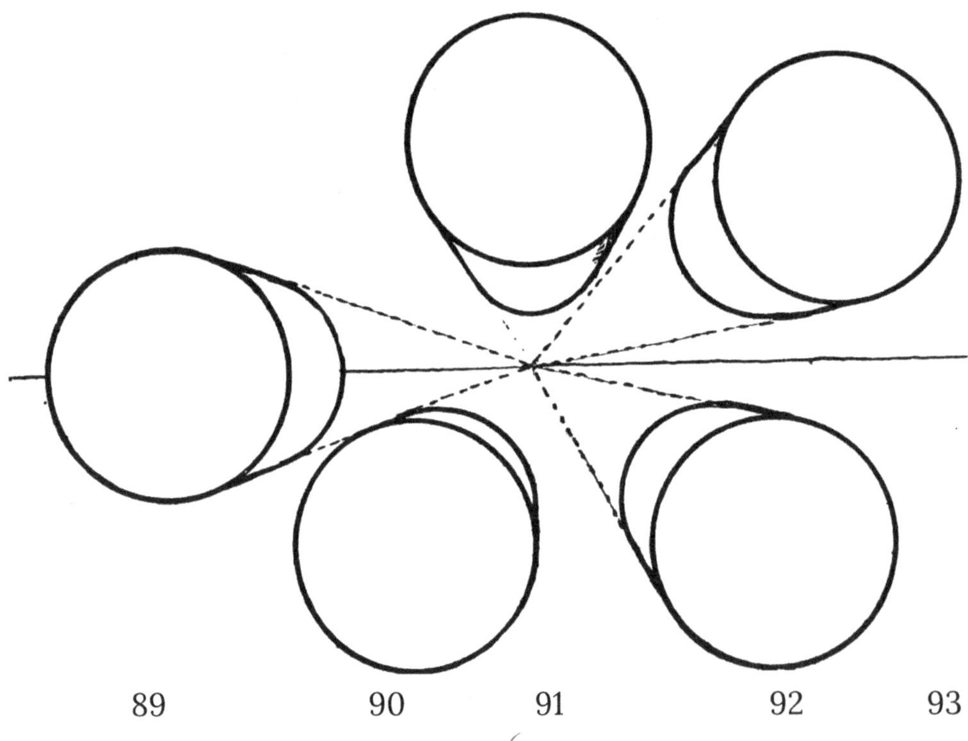

89   90   91   92   93

(5) Draw a horizon line on the blackboard and in it mark a center of vision.

(6) Ask what each represents.

(7) Hold the receding cylinder with one end flat against the blackboard and over the center of vision. How much of the cylinder can be seen in this position?

(8) Place the cylinder against the blackboard at the right, the left, above, and below the center of vision, all the time drilling the class with questions.

(9) Around a center of vision draw five receding cylinders and let the class draw similar ones.

(10) Drill with the class at the board. Draw a receding cylinder below the eye, above the eye, at the right of the eye, at the left of the eye, below and at the right of the eye, etc.

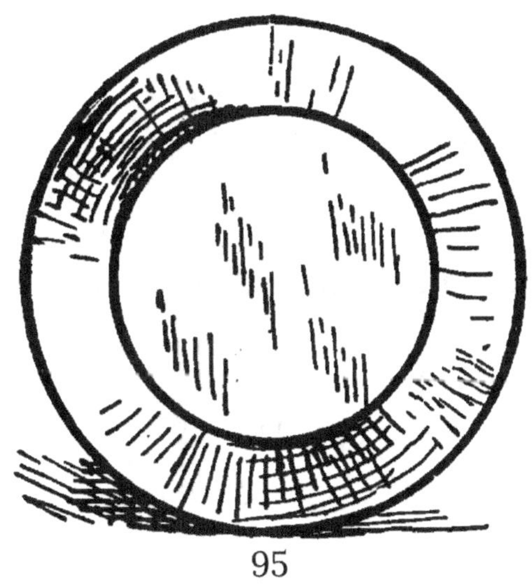

95

FIGURE 95. – (1) Hold a fruit can with the open end towards the class. How many edges can you see? Can you see a plane face in the cylinder? Can you see a curved face?

(2) Walter may take the pointer and point to the edges. Point to a curved face, a plane face.

(3) Draw the hollow cylinder on the blackboard as in Fig. 95, and let the class draw a similar one.

(4) Drill the class at the blackboard by drawing Fig. 95 in various positions about the center of vision: below and above the eye, at the right and left of the eye, below and at the left and right, and above and at the left and right.

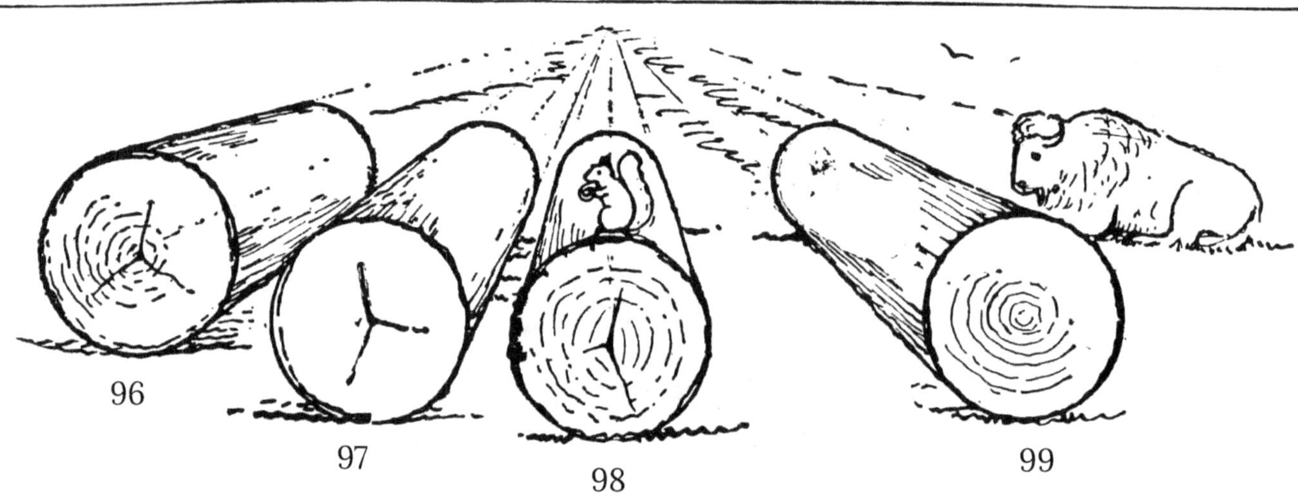

FIGURE 96 – 99. – (1) Draw a horizon line and in it mark a center of vision. Ask what each represents.

(2) Below and at the left of the center of vision, draw logs 96 and 97; below the center of vision, draw log 98; and below and at the right, draw log 99.

(3) Let the class draw similar logs.

(4) Drill the class at the blackboard. Charles may draw a log below and at the left of the eye. Mollie may draw one below the eye. Blanche may draw one below and at the right of the eye. All may draw three logs: one below and at the left, one below, and one below and at the right.

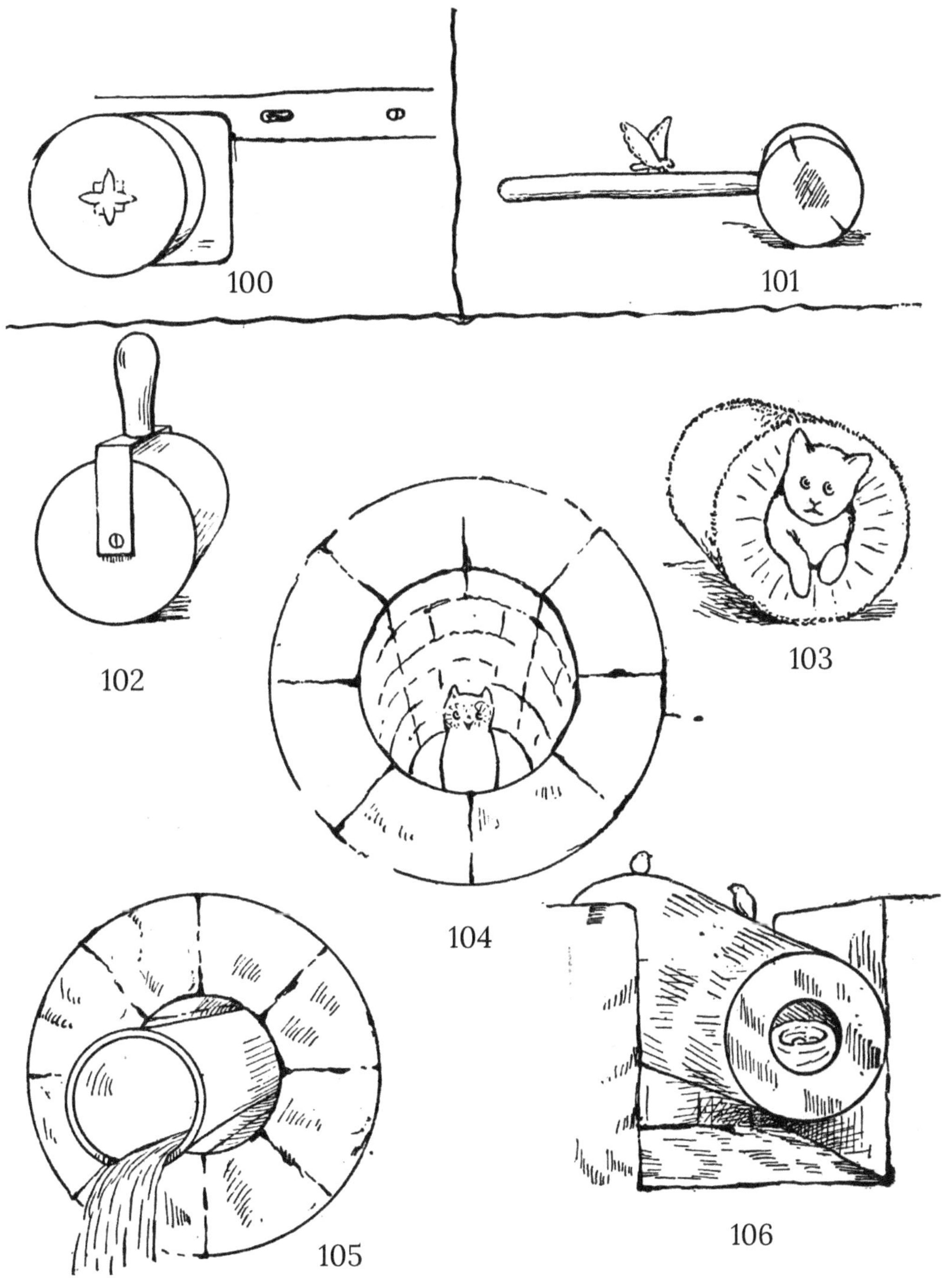

100

101

102

104

103

105

106

APPLICATIONS OF THE RECEDING CYLINDER

FIGURE 100 - 106. – are simple applications of the receding cylinder as applied to familiar forms. These applications may be multiplied indefinitely. Nearly all of the forms that resemble the cylinder may be drawn in all three divisions of the cylinder, viz.: vertical, horizontal, and receding, and it is an excellent practice to draw the various applications of the cylinder in these positions as well as in positions in regard to the eye. For example, the muff, Fig. 103, may be drawn in nine positions in regard to the eye and also in the three positions of the cylinder. It is better to draw one object in these various positions than many objects in one position.

Figure 100 is a cap on a peg. Fig. 101 is a mallet. Fig. 102 is a roller, and Fig. 103 is a muff.

Figure 104 is an application of the inside of a hollow cylinder above the level of the eye. It is a window or opening through a wall. Fig. 105 is a similar application below and at the left of the eye.

The lines that represent the sides of the cannon in Fig. 106 do not converge to a point because they are not parallel.

The following problems are for drill work in the class, and also to give suggestions to the teacher in applying her work to the needs of the class.

EASY PROBLEMS IN THE CYLINDER.

(1) Draw Fig. 100 at the right of the eye.

(2) Draw Fig. 100 as a horizontal cylinder at the left of the eye, at the right of the eye, and as a vertical cylinder below the eye.

(3) Find the center of vision in Fig. 100, Fig. 101, Fig. 102, Fig. 103, Fig. 104, and Fig. 105.

(4) Draw Fig. 101 as a horizontal cylinder and as a vertical cylinder.

(5) Draw Fig. 102 as a horizontal cylinder at the left of the eye, below, and at the right of the eye.

(6) Draw Fig. 103 below and at the left of the eye, below the eye, at the left of the eye, in front of the eye, at the right of the eye, as a horizontal cylinder, and as a vertical cylinder.

(7) Draw Fig. 104 below the eye, at the right of the eye, at the left of the eye, and below and at the left of the eye, as a horizontal cylinder and as a vertical cylinder.

(8) Draw Fig. 105 below the eye and below and at the right of the eye.

(9) Draw Fig. 22 as a horizontal cylinder, Fig. 24 as a horizontal cylinder, and as a receding cylinder.

(10) Draw Fig. 37 as a horizontal cylinder.

(11) Draw Fig. 43 as a horizontal cylinder.

(12) Draw the logs in Fig. 71 as receding cylinders.

(13) Draw a horizontal and receding log. Also, draw two stumps. Combine the same drawing.

(14) Draw Fig. 72 as a receding cylinder.

(15) Draw Fig. 74 as a vertical cylinder.

(16) Draw Fig. 76 as a receding cylinder.

THE HEMISPHERE.

The hemisphere is similar to the cylinder in principle and may be studied in the same manner.

Use for a model a hemisphere modeled from clay or cut from plaster. A croquet ball split in halves makes a very good model.

Divide the study of the hemisphere into two parts: (1) When the base is downward as in Figs. 107, 108, and 111, and (2) When the base is upward as in Figs. 109 and 110.

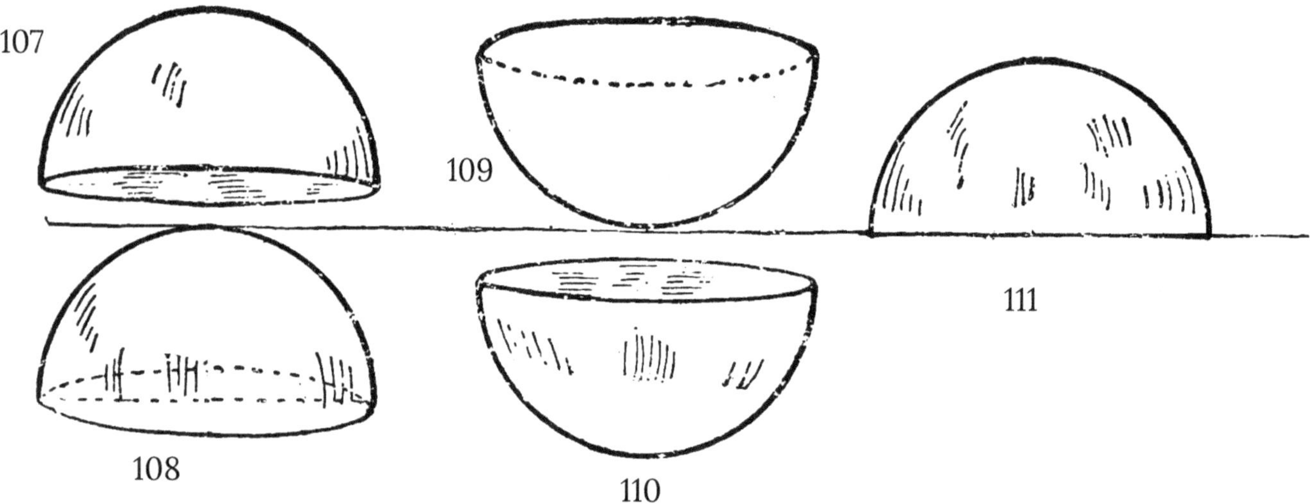

Drill the class as in the vertical cylinder.

Hold the hemisphere in the hand with the base down. Lead the class to see (1) that when the base is below the eye, it cannot be seen, but the edge curves downward as in the base of the vertical cylinder below the eye (see Fig. 108). (2) That when the base is above the eye, it can be seen as in Fig. 107. (3) That when the base is on a level with the eye, it is represented by a horizontal line as in Fig. 111.

Turn the hemisphere over so that the base will be upward. (1) Lead the pupils to see that when the base is below the eye, it can be seen (Fig. 110). (2) When above the eye, it cannot be seen as in Fig. 109. (3) When on a level with the eye, the base will be represented by a horizontal line.

Draw a horizon line on the board. Ask what it represents. Hold the hemisphere above this line with the base down and ask if it can be seen. Do the same below the line and on a level with the line. Draw Figs. from 107 to 111 on the board and let the class draw similar ones.

Drill the class at the blackboard. Alice may draw a hemisphere with the base downward below the level of the eye. Draw the same with the base upward. Eliza may draw a hemisphere above the eye with the base downward and with the base upward. Harry may draw a hemisphere with the base downward and on a level with the eye, and with the base upward and on a level with the eye.

FIGURE 112 - 114. – (1) Draw a hat on the blackboard with the rim above the eye, below the eye, and on a level with the eye.

(2) Mollie may take a hat and hold it in the same position before her eye as the hat above the level of the eye, below the level of the eye, and on a level with the eye.

(3) Let the class make similar drawings.

112

113

114

115

116

117

118

(4) Drill at the blackboard. Let each pupil draw a hat above the eye and change it to a hat below the eye. Draw a hat on a level with the eye. Draw a hat below the eye and change it into one above the eye.

FIGURE 115 - 118. are simple applications of the hemisphere, each of which may be modified indefinitely by placing them at various positions in regard to the level of the eye.

THE CONE.

The cone is the same as the hemisphere with the exception of the apex, which is directly over the center of the base.

Use for a model a cone modeled from clay, cut or molded from plaster of Paris, or made out of cardboard.

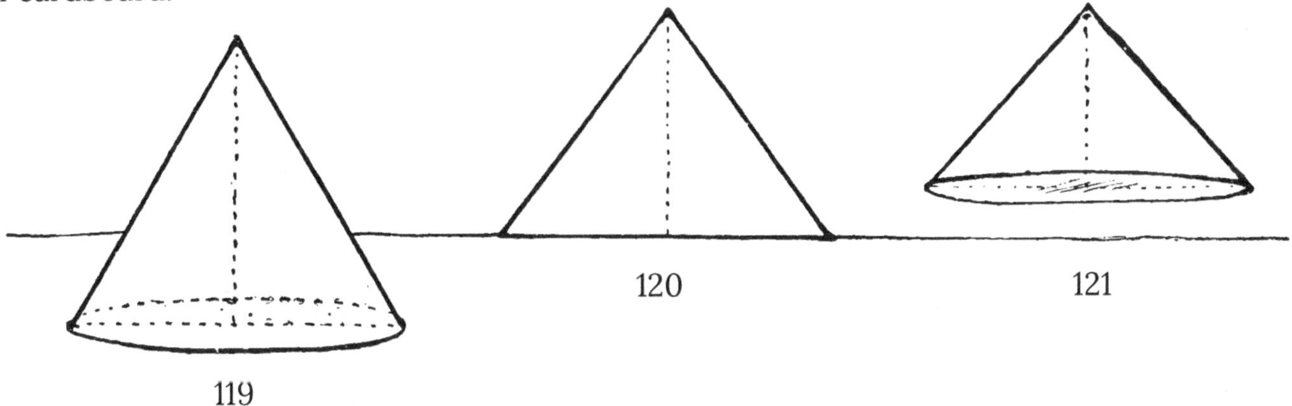

FIGURE 119 - 121. – Study it below, above, and on a level with the eye, as in Figs. 119-121, also by inverting them the same as in the hemisphere.

FIGURE 122 - 126. – are simple applications of the cone.

EASY PROBLEMS.

(1) Change Fig. 112 into a conical hat. Fig. 114. Fig. 113.

(2) Turn Fig. 114 so that the open part will be up.

(3) Draw Fig. 115 below the eye, resting on the cut-off part.

(4) Draw Fig. 116 with the base of the hive on a level with the eye.

(5) Draw Fig. 117 with the horizon line even with the top of the posts.

(6) Draw a conical pile of potatoes, melons, pears, and pumpkins.

(7) Turn Fig. 123 into a pile like a hemisphere.

122

123

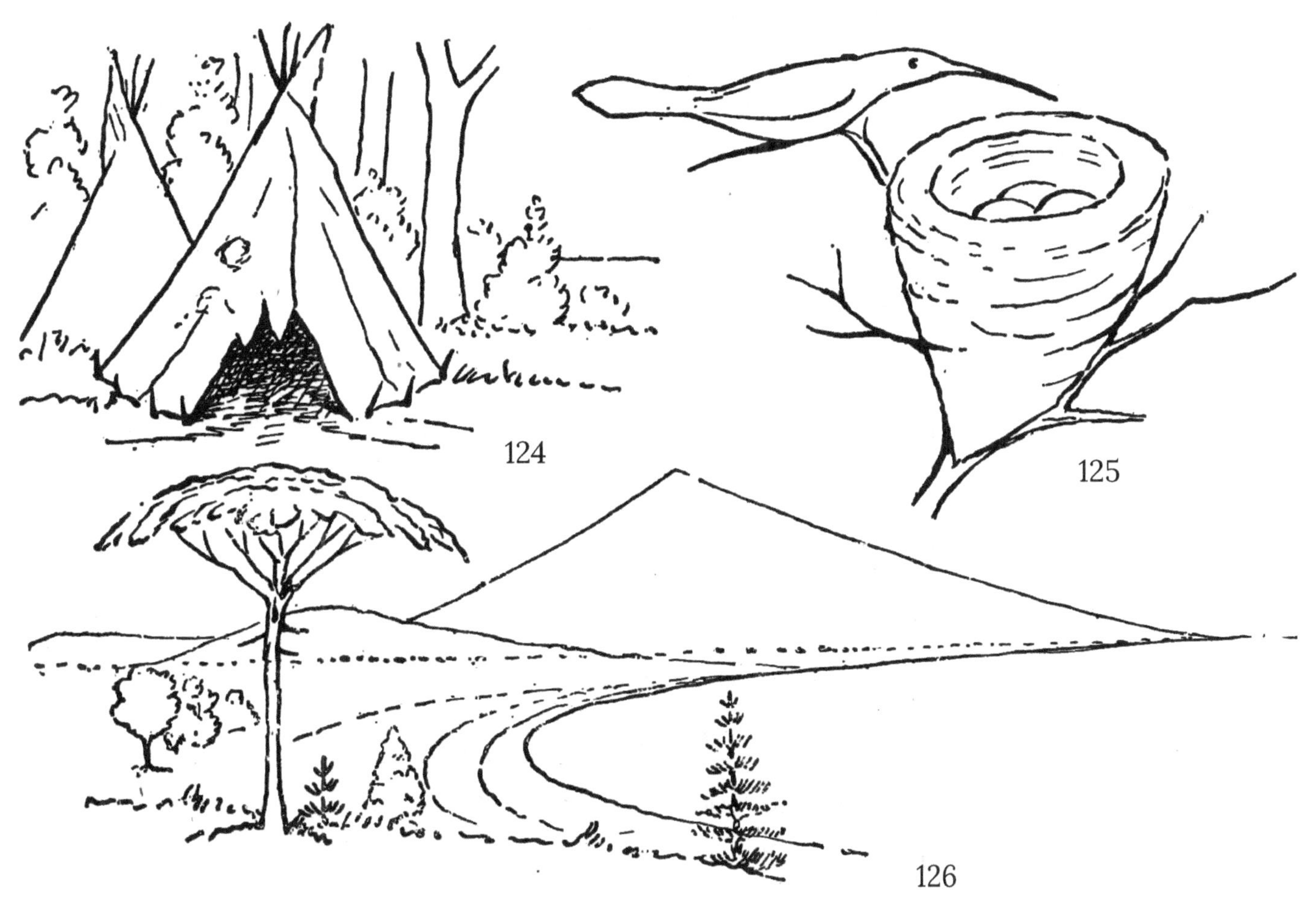

124

125

126

OBJECTS BASED ON THE TYPE FORMS.

Many of these objects may be based on one or more type forms according to their shape. For example, a basket may be based on the cube, the cylinder, or the hemisphere, according to its shape.

THE CUBE.

wall	bed	house	trough
chair	boat-house	sign	chest
barn	beehive	trunk	shed
bureau	stone	cabin	book-case
door	hut	stand	window
shanty	piano	wood-pile	organ
wood-house	table	safe	book
bar of soap	basket	monument	chimney
bird-house	wharf	coffee-mill	punt
cross	scow	block-house	fort
stockade	trap	steps	cage
hen-coop	tent	tower	fence
fountain	wagon	vase	cart
bottles	bridge	mallet	cab
heater	coach	head-light	car
pump			

LIKE THE INSIDE OF THE CUBE.

well   room   tunnel   fire-place   hall   shaft

LIKE THE TOP FACE OF THE CUBE.

bay   park   avenue   lake

grass-plat road   road   island   pond

path   lot   yard   pavement

pen

CYLINDER.

grind-stone   cannon   dipper   window

mortar   bucket   basket   drum

bowl   chinney   tambourine   log

fort   cymbals   churn   trap

hour-glass   flowers   cage   crown

spool   bridge   horn   pipe

monument   turret   buoy   hydrant

capstan	sieve	cross	lantern
can	column	lamp	cheese-box
tower	bull's eye	bag full	light-house
kettle	cuspidore	fountain	pans
firkin	vase	cups	bicycle
wheels	mugs	mallet	barrel
bottles	rolling-pin	keg	pails
peck	jar	duster	stove
jug	post	heater	tub
head	shawl-strap	hat	tent
demijohn	cap	ring	cigar
muff	nest	goblet	electric-light
clock	money	pump	pint
candle	roll of paper	scroll	rocket
roller	banjo	bay	cuff
button	grass-plat	well	island
lake	pond		

SPHERE.

apple	pear	egg	monument
cherry	orange	peach	pumpkin
melon	ball	marble	currants
gooseberry	rose	pear	egg
plum	lemon	squash	potato
turnip	onion	strawberry	ballon
head	tea-pot	tree	moon
sun	snow-ball	grape	acorn
haystack	cocoanut	gourd	bead
knot	cannon-ball	bullet	wasp's nest

HEMISPHERE.

bee-hive	trunk	window	basket
trap	wagon top	bridge	wood-pile
fire-place	arch	vase	drum
kettle	flowers	hat	cap
1-2 apple	1-2 pumpkin	toad stool	dome
Esquimau-hut	bowl	lamp-shade	call-bell
fish-net	umbrella	hay stack	mountain
hill			

CONE.

cage	tent	wood-pile	monument
vase	flower	buoy	cuspidore
hat	cap	duster	bird's nest
wasp's nest	toad-stool	lamp-shade	bell
fish-nest	hay-stack	mountain	ink-bottle
funnel	top	fool's cap	radish
carrot	fish	house-top	wigwam

PRISM.

boat-house	sign	book	window
shed	cabin	fort	bridge
wood-pile	fire-place	fountain	vase
bottle	pond	bay	island
grass plat	field	roofs	hen-coop
oil-can	pyramid	pig's trough	cheese house
base ball diamond			

PART IV.

INVENTION

There are three simple methods of invention: (1) Invention by line, (2) Invention by form, (3) Invention by idea[10].

INVENTION BY LINES.

There are two classes of lines: (1) straight, (2) curved.

Straight lines are divided into (1) vertical, (2) horizontal, (3) oblique.

Curved lines are divided into (1) vertically curved, (2) horizontally curved, (3) obliquely curved.

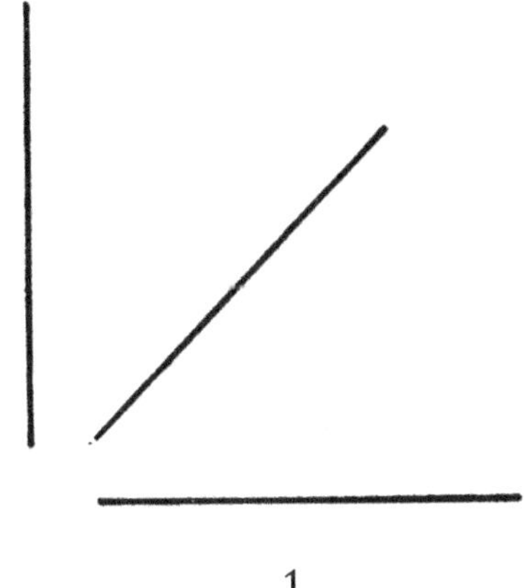

1

FIGURE 1. – represents the vertical, horizontal, and oblique lines.

10   Invention by idea is omitted, as being too complicated for elementary drawing

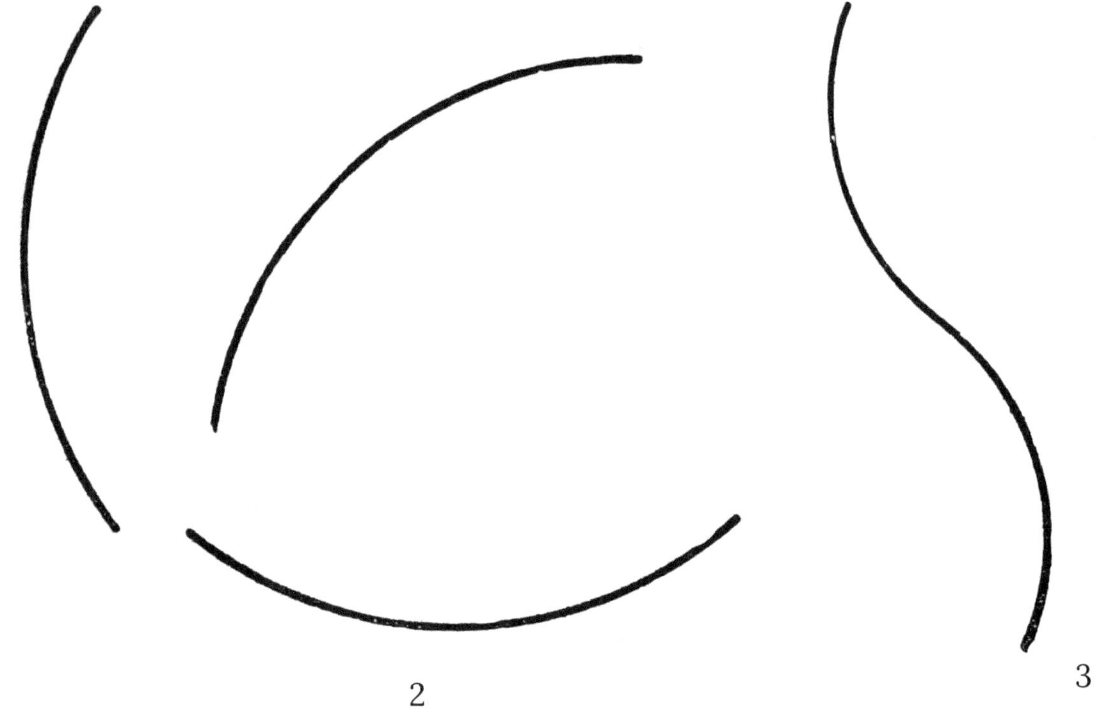

2　　　　　　　　　　　　3

FIGURE 2. – represents the vertically curved, horizontally curved, and obliquely curved lines.

FIGURE 3. – represents the *double* curve, which may be vertical, horizontal, or oblique.

When the curved lines represented by Fig. 2 curve outward, they are called *outward curves* (A and B, Fig. 5), and when inward, they are called *inward curves* (A and B, Fig. 6).

Teach these different kinds of lines to the class.

(1) Hold the pointer vertically before the class. Horizontally. Obliquely. Lead the class to

recognize each position. (2) John, you may take the pointer. Hold it vertically. Horizontally. Obliquely. (3) Make a vertical movement with your hand. What kind of a movement did I make? Make a horizontal. An oblique. (4) All may stand. Make a vertical movement with your hand. A horizontal movement. An oblique movement. (5) You may all draw an oblique line on your tablets. A vertical line. A horizontal line. (6) Drill the class at the black-board.

Teach the vertical, horizontal, and oblique curves in the same manner, also the double curves.[11]

There are three methods of inventing by line: (1) by dictation, (2) by substitution, (3) by design.

LINE DICTATION.

In line dictation, the pupils draw line for line that which is dictated to them by the teacher.

The black-board is the proper place for this work, though the tablet may be used if the black-board cannot.

Each measurement should be made with the unaided eye and each line drawn with the unaided hand.

The method is as follows: Class at the black-board. Teacher dictates.

11   Part of a barrel hoop may be used instead of the pointer when teaching the curves.

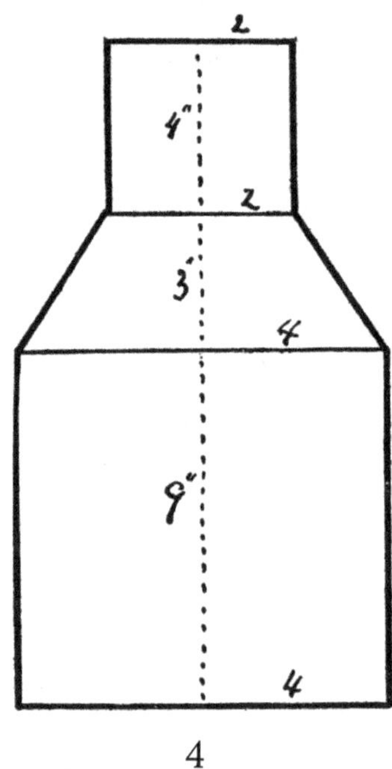

4

FIGURE 4. – (1) Draw a light vertical line 16^{12} long. This is called the median line. (2) Through the upper extremity of the median line, draw a horizontal line projecting 2" on each side. (3) 4" below this horizontal line, draw another horizontal line like it. (4) 3" below the last horizontal line, draw a horizontal line projecting 4" on each side of the median line. (5) Through the lower extremity of the median line, draw a horizontal line like the last one. (6) Connect the extremities of the first and second horizontal lines by vertical lines. (7) Connect the extremities of the second and third horizontal lines with oblique lines. (8) Connect the extremities of the third and last horizontal lines with vertical lines.

12   One indice stands for feet, and two indices for inches. It may be necessary to teach the length of an inch and of a foot in the class. Accuracy in these measurements is not to be expected at first, nor is it necessary. Practice and comparison will give accuracy.

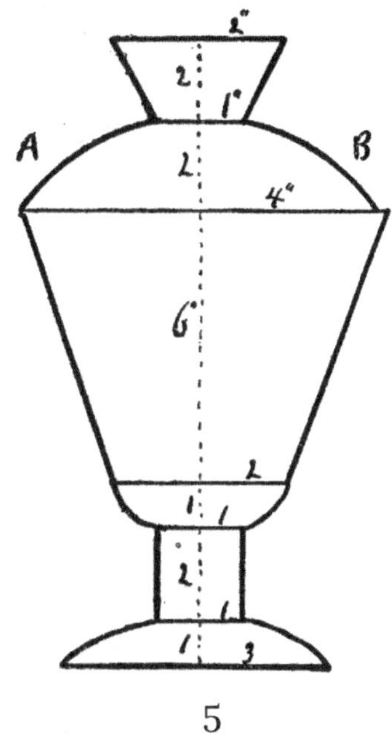

5

FIGURE 5. – (1) Draw a light vertical median line 14" long. (2) Through the upper extremity of the median line, draw a horizontal line projecting 2" on each side. (3) 2" below this last line, draw a horizontal line projecting 1" on each side of the median line. (4) 2" below this last line, draw a horizontal line projecting 4" on each side of the median line. (5) 6" below the last line, draw a horizontal line projecting 2" on each side of the median line. (6) 1' below the last line, draw a horizontal line projecting 1" on each side of the median line. (7) Draw a similar line 2" below the last. (8) Through the lower extremity of the median line, draw a horizontal line projecting 3" on each side. (9) Connect the extremities of the first and second lines with oblique lines, the second and third with outward curved lines, the third and fourth with oblique lines, the fourth and fifth with outward curves, the fifth and sixth with vertical lines, and the sixth and last with outward curves.

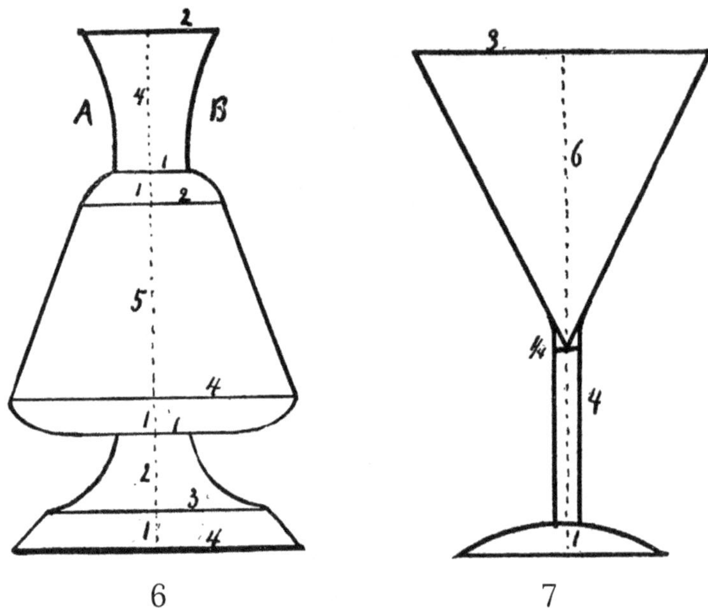

6   7

FIGURE 6. – (1) Draw lightly a vertical median line 14" long. (2) Beginning with the upper extremity of the median line, draw horizontal lines 4", 1", 5", 1", 2", and 1" apart, projecting in the order given 2", 1", 2", 4", 1", 3", and 4" on each side of the median line. (3) Connect the extremities of the first and second horizontal lines with inward curves, the second and third with outward curves, the third and fourth with oblique lines, the fourth and fifth with outward curves, the fifth and sixth with inward curves, and the sixth and last with oblique lines.

FIGURE 7. – (1) Draw a light vertical median line 11" long. (2) Beginning at the upper extremity of the median line, draw horizontal lines 6", 4", and 1" apart and projecting in the order given 3", 1", 1", and 2" on each side of the median line. (3) Connect the extremities of the first and second horizontal lines with oblique lines, the second and third with vertical lines, and the third and last with outward curves.

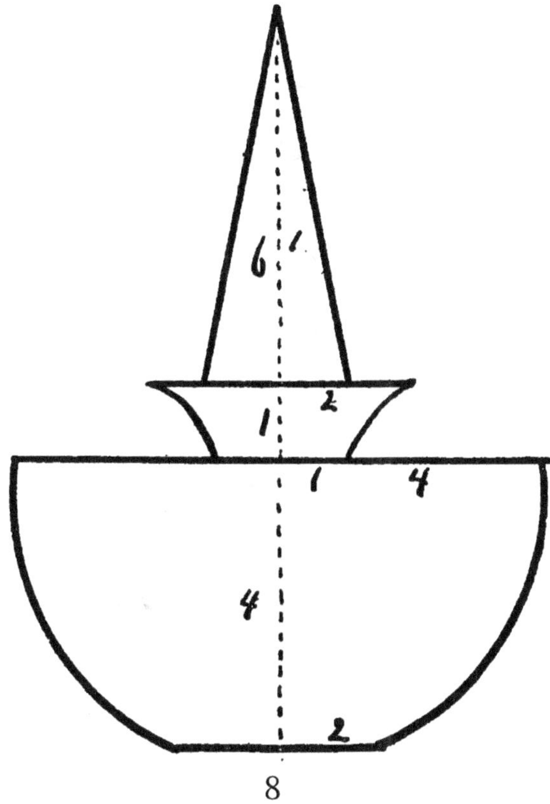

FIGURE 8. – (1) Draw a light vertical median line 11" long. (2) Beginning at the upper extremity of the median line, place points 6", 1", and 4" apart, and through them draw horizontal lines projecting 0", 2", 4", and 2" on each side of the median line. (3) In the first and second horizontal lines, place points 1" on each side of the median line. (4) Connect the upper extremity of the median line and the points in the first horizontal line with oblique lines, the extremities of the first horizontal line and the points in the second horizontal line with inward curves, and the extremities of the remaining horizontal lines with outward curves.

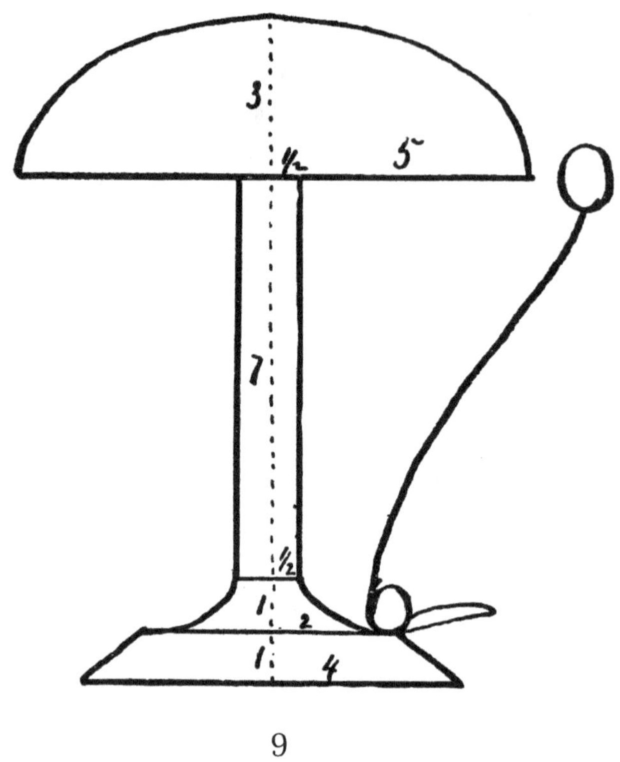

FIGURE 9. – (1) Draw a light vertical median line 12" long. (2) Beginning at the upper extremity of the median line, place points 3", 7", 1", and 1" apart, and through them draw horizontal lines projecting 0", 5", 1", 2", and 4" on each side of the median line. (3) In the first horizontal line, place points 1/2 on each side of the median line. (4) Connect the upper extremity of the median line and the extremities of the first horizontal line with outward curves, the points in the first horizontal line and the extremities of the second horizontal line with vertical lines, the second and third horizontal lines with inward curves, the third and last with oblique lines. (5) 1/2 at the right of the first horizontal line, and at the right extremity of the third horizontal

line, draw circles. (6) Connect these circles with a double curve. (7) Tangent to the lower and outer circumference of the second circle, draw a horizontal line 1" long.

Nearly all common forms can be dictated. To such a degree of accuracy can this be carried that a human face can be dictated and drawn by a well-drilled class.

LINE SUBSTITUTION.

By line substitution, the shape of a given object is changed or modified by *substituting the different kinds of straight and curved lines in place of existing lines.*

For example, the object to be designed is a goblet. The goblet is naturally divided into three sections: (1) The bowl, (2) the stem, (3) the standard.

The teacher draws a simple type on the black-board with vertical and horizontal lines similar to Fig. 10. From this type, the pupils invent an indefinite number of goblets by substituting for the vertical lines of Fig. 10 the various kinds of straight and curved lines, making goblets similar to Figs. 11 - 21.

For the vertical lines in Fig. 10, outward vertical curves are substituted in Fig. 11; inward vertical curves in Fig. 12; and double vertical curves in Fig. 13.

For the vertical lines in Fig. 10, oblique lines slanting outward at the top have been substituted in Fig. 14; oblique outward curves in Fig. 15; oblique inward curves in Fig. 16; and oblique double curves in Fig. 17.

For the vertical lines of Fig. 10, oblique lines slanting inward at the top have been substituted in Fig. 18; oblique inward curves in Fig. 19; oblique outward curves in Fig. 20; and oblique double curves in Fig. 21.

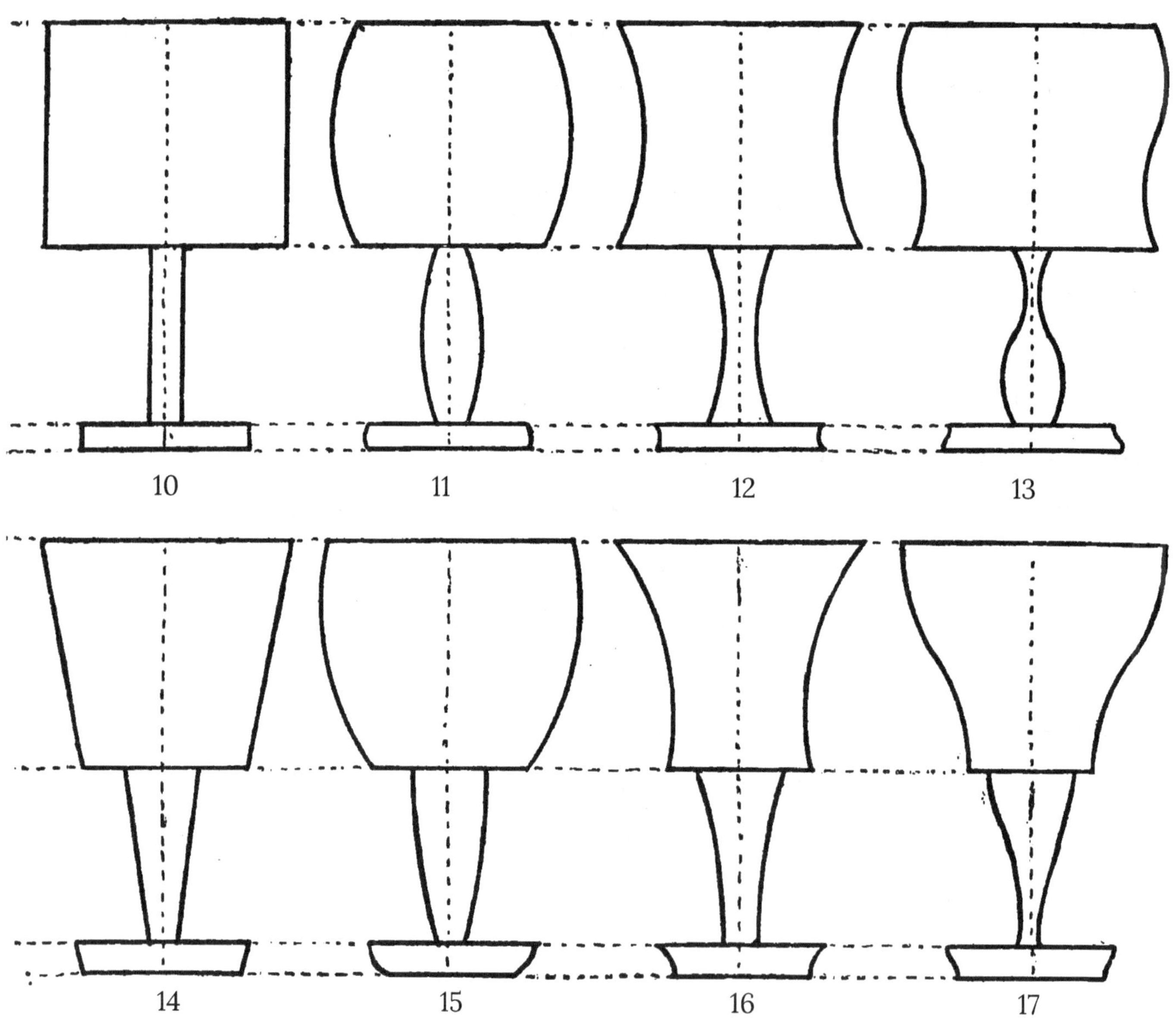

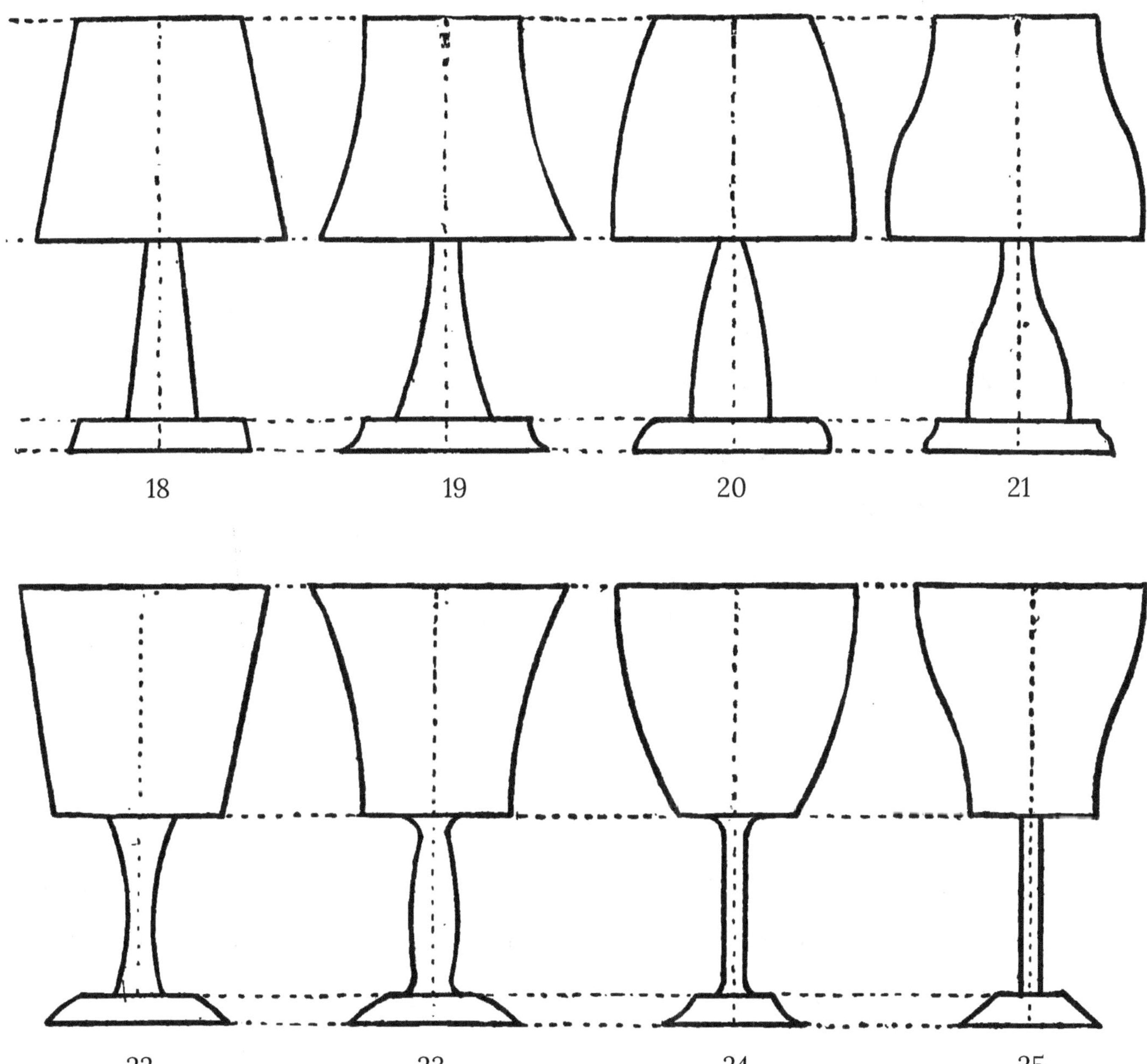

18
19
20
21
22
23
24
25

In the examples thus far given, the same kind of line is used in each goblet. By combining two or more kinds of lines in the same goblet, there is practically no end to the combinations that can be made.

For example, in Fig. 22, the oblique line, the inward curve, and the outward curve are combined. In Fig. 23, the inward curve and two outward curves are combined. In Fig. 24, the outward curve, the vertical line, and the inward curve are combined, and in Fig. 25, the double curve, the vertical line, and the oblique line are combined.

The method of inventing by substitution may be taught as follows: (1) Draw a simple type of the object to be designed on the black-board. (2) Let the class copy. (3) Divide the object into as many sections as there are angles on the side of the object. (4) Divide these sections by light horizontal lines similar to the dotted lines in the examples. These lines may be drawn with a straight edge or rule. (5) Draw the median line and design the objects.

DESIGNING BY LINE.

Designing by line includes line substitution. In substitution, the lines in corresponding sections are of the same vertical height, but in design, they may be changed in vertical height and the horizontal lines changed in length as well, thus changing the proportion.

Substitution changes the *kind of line. Design the kind of line and its length.*

Thus, section A in Fig. 32, which is the type form, is short; in Fig. 36, it is long; and in Fig. 40, it is wide. In Fig. 36, the vertical lengths have been changed, and in Fig. 40, both the vertical and horizontal lengths have been changed.

The horizontal rows of vases are made by substitution, the vertical rows by design.

The second horizontal row is designed from the first horizontal row by changing the vertical length of the sections.

The third horizontal row is designed from the first horizontal row by changing the vertical length of the sections and their width.

A very good way to teach the method is as follows: (1) Draw a simple type of the object to be designed on the black-board, similar to Fig. 32. (2) Let the class draw by substitution a row of four of the objects from the type given, similar to Figs. 32 - 35. (3) Let the class draw a second row by design from the first row, changing the vertical length of the sections, similar to Figs. 36–39. (4) Let the class draw a third row by design from the first row, by changing the width of the sections. (5) Let the class draw a fourth row by design from the first row, changing both the vertical length and the width of the sections. (6) Let the class draw a fifth row, blending both substitution and design as fancy may direct.

All forms, however complicated, may be changed or modified by substitution and design. Figs. 26 - 31 are simple examples showing how the face may be changed by these two methods. The heads are the same in shape; the nose and mouth alone are changed. In Figs. 26, 27, and

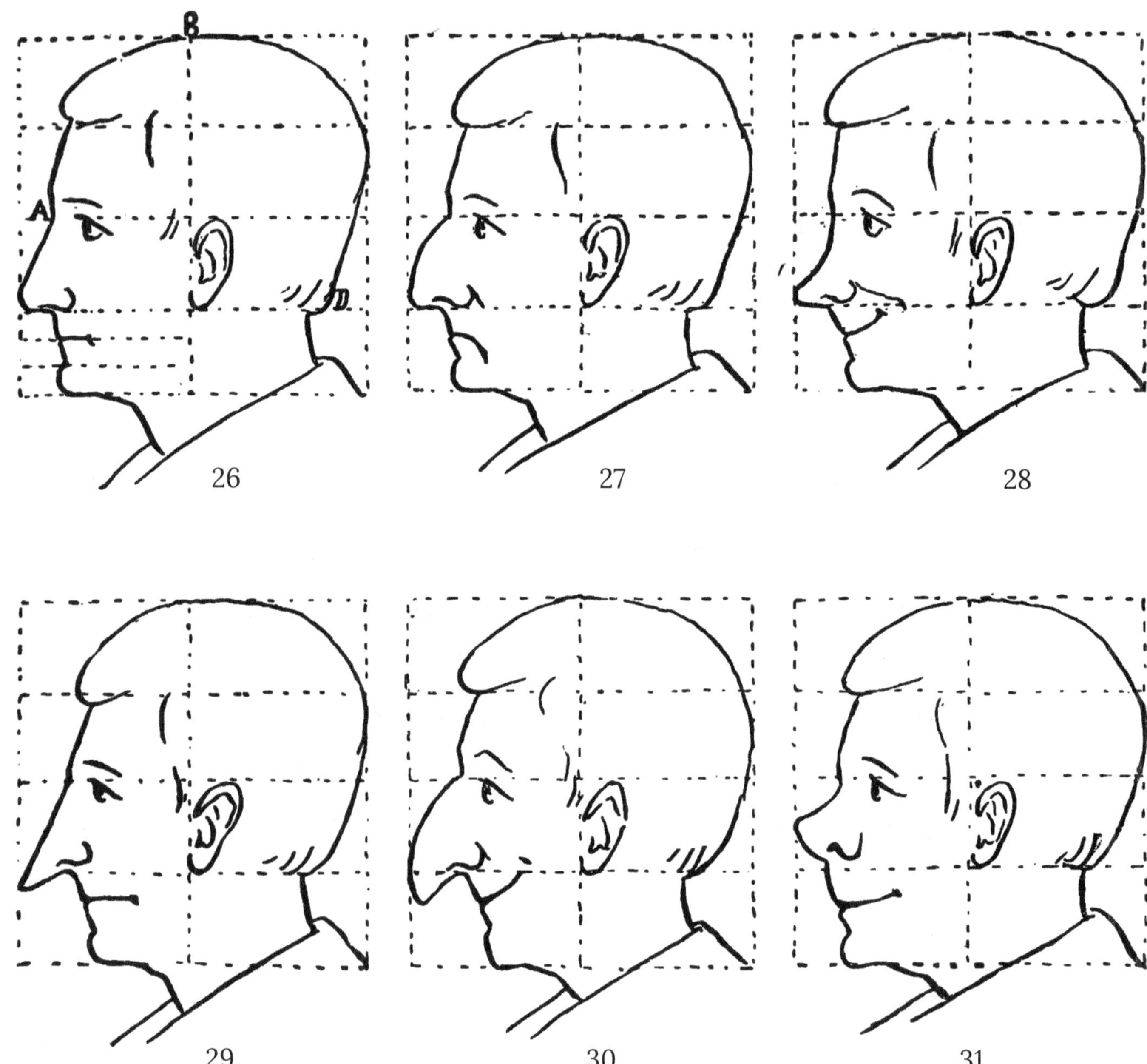

26

27

28

29

30

31

28, the nose and mouth are changed by substitution; in Figs. 29, 30, and 31 by design.

FIGURE 26. – A well-shaped human head, viewed in profile, is as long from the end of the nose to the back of the head, as from the bottom of the chin to the top of the head, and is contained in a square. See Fig. 26.

Observe that the root of the nose, the upper eyelid, and the top of the ear are on the horizontal line halfway between the chin and the top of the head, and that the end of the nose, the lower part of the ear, and the base of the brain are on the horizontal line marking the first quarter from the bottom.

The profile may be drawn as follows: (Fig. 26). (1) Draw a square. (2) Divide the square horizontally into four equal parts and vertically into two equal parts. (3) Divide the lower quarter on the side of the face into three equal parts. (4) Choose the point A and through the points B and C to D, draw as near a circle as possible. The point C is halfway between the two horizontal lines. The point D is about one-third the distance to the median line from the side of the square. (5) Draw the nose. (6) Draw the mouth and chin. (7) Draw the ear and neck. (8) Substitute for the oblique line of the nose and the horizontal line of the mouth in Fig. 26 an outward curved nose and a downward curved mouth as in Fig. 27. (9) Substitute for the straight nose and mouth in Fig. 26 the inward curved nose and upward curved mouth in Fig. 28. (10) Lengthen out the nose and mouth of Fig. 26 to make Fig. 29. (11) Lengthen out the nose of Fig. 27 and turn the mouth upward for Fig. 30. (12) Shorten the nose of Fig. 28 and make the mouth long for Fig. 31.

Other features may be changed in the same manner.

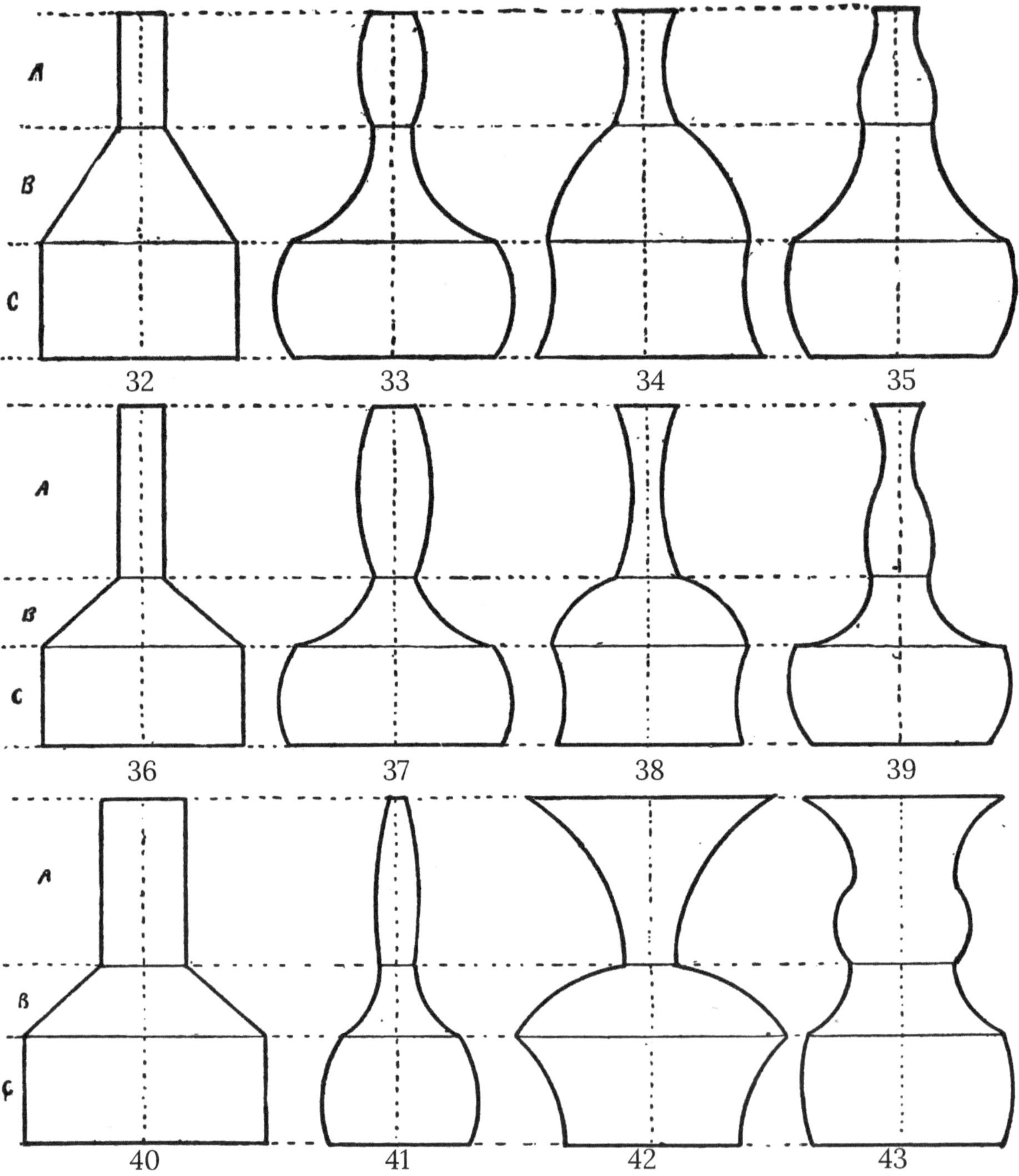

A
B
C
32
33
34
35
A
B
C
36
37
38
39
A
B
C
40
41
42
43

INVENTION BY FORM.

Invention by form includes invention by line. In place of the line, the whole form enclosed by the line is considered. The form is used in place of the line.

First of all, the most common figures and forms must be taught. They are the triangle, square, rectangle, circle, ellipse, oval (Fig. 44), pear (Fig. 45), acorn (Fig. 46), heart (Fig. 47), ovoid (Fig. 48), crescent (Fig. 49), balloon (Fig. 50), kidney (Fig. 51), bell (Fig. 52), keystone (Fig. 53), shield (Fig. 54), diamond (Fig. 55), lens (Fig. 56), funnel (Fig. 57), lance (Fig. 58), kite (Fig. 59), arrow (Fig. 60), fan (Fig. 61), semicircle (Fig. 62), umbrella (Fig. 63).

Cut from cardboard three of each of these figures and place them in the box used for that purpose. Cut each one of different size and shape. For example, cut a long acorn, a broad acorn, and a medium acorn.

These forms may be taught in the class as follows: (1) If possible, show the actual form to the class. If that is not possible, use the cardboard figure. For example, hold an acorn before the class and, by means of questions, impress that form on their minds. (2) Draw an outline of the acorn on the blackboard for the class to copy. (3) John may find three figures shaped like an acorn in the box and hold them before the class. (4) Draw a broad, a long, and a medium acorn upon the blackboard and let the class draw similar ones. (5) Draw an acorn on the blackboard with the apex pointing upward, to the right, to the left, and let the class draw similar ones. (6) Drill with the class at the blackboard. Draw a long acorn, a broad acorn, a medium acorn, and an acorn with the apex pointing upward, downward, to the right, to the left, etc. In like man-

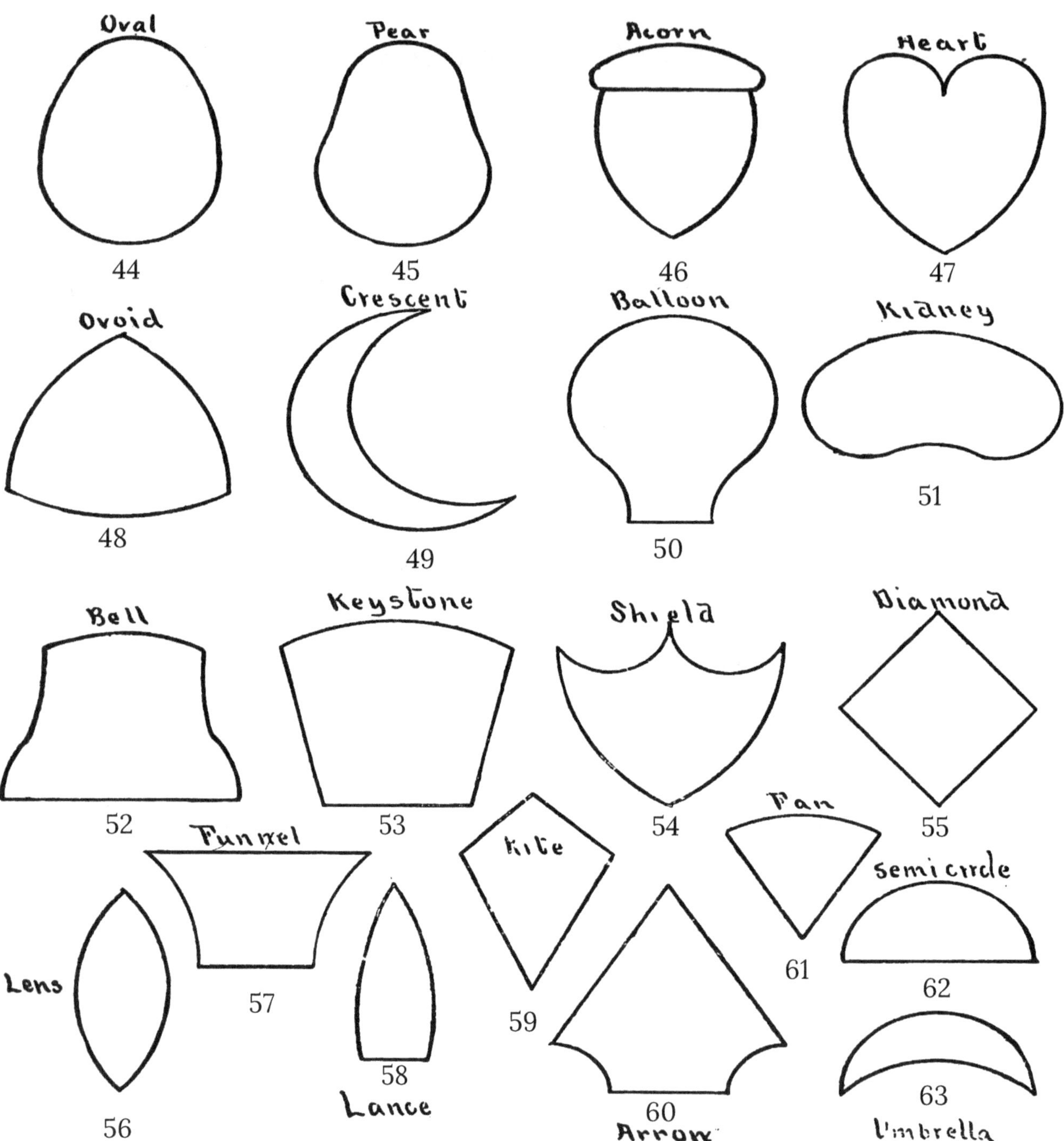

Oval
Pear
Acorn
Heart
44
45
46
47
Ovoid
Crescent
Balloon
Kidney
48
49
50
51
Bell
Keystone
Shield
Diamond
52
53
54
55
Funnel
Kite
Fan
Semicircle
Lens
57
58
59
61
62
56
Lance
60
63
Arrow
Umbrella

ner, teach each form.

A very interesting way of reviewing these forms is as follows: (1) The class may stand. (2) Place the forefinger of each hand together and elevate them somewhat above the head and mark in the air each form, marking half the form with each finger, and letting the class name the form you mark out. (3) Let each one in the class mark out the form together as you call for them. (4) Drill at the blackboard.

Invention by form, the same as invention by lines, is divided into (1) form dictation, (2) form substitution, (3) form design.

FORM DICTATION.

Form dictation follows line dictation. In form dictation, the pupil chooses his own lines to enclose the form dictated to him.

Form dictation should be taught with the class at the blackboard.

This method is followed when drilling the class on the forms, Figs. 44 - 63. When you tell the class to draw a long acorn, it is form dictation.

It is an excellent practice, when teaching the forms, to dictate the size as well as the shape, thus:

FIGURE 64. – Draw a keystone 9" wide and 12" high.

FIGURE 65. – Draw a keystone 16" wide and 4" high.

FIGURE 66. – Draw a horizontal lens 18" long and 5" thick.

FIGURE 67. – Draw a vertical lens 12" long and 3" thick.

FIGURE 68. – Draw a vertical lens 8" long and 4" thick.

FIGURE 69. – Draw a horizontal half lens 12" long and 2" thick.

FIGURE 70. – Draw a horizontal half lens 24" long and 3" thick.

When dictating an object containing more than one form, name the object first, and then dictate each part separately, thus:

FIGURE 71 - 74. – (1) Draw a wine glass with a semi-circular bowl.

(2) A plain rectangular stem.

(3) And a standard shaped like a half lens.

(4) Add a circular ornament to the stem near the middle part.

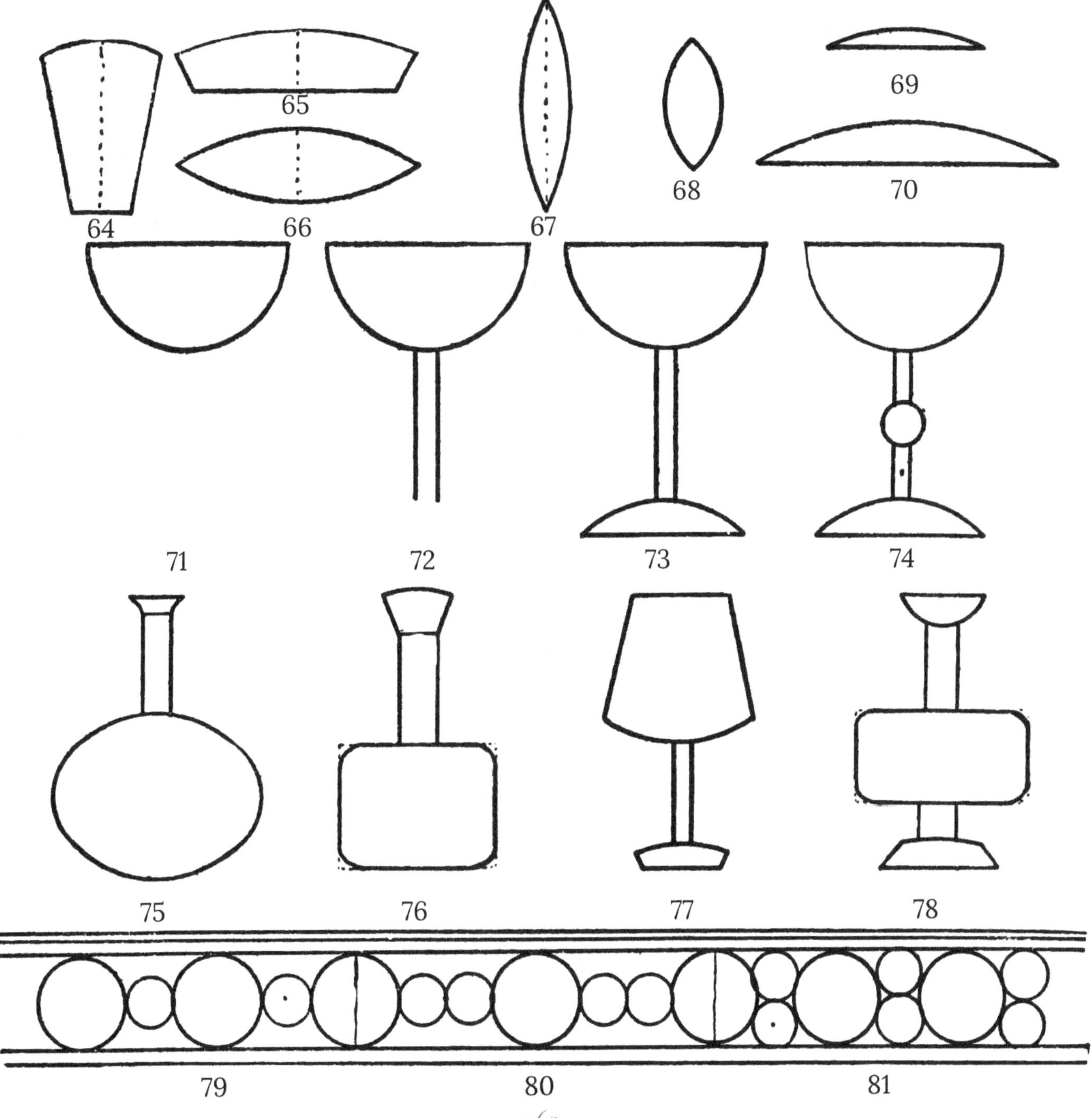

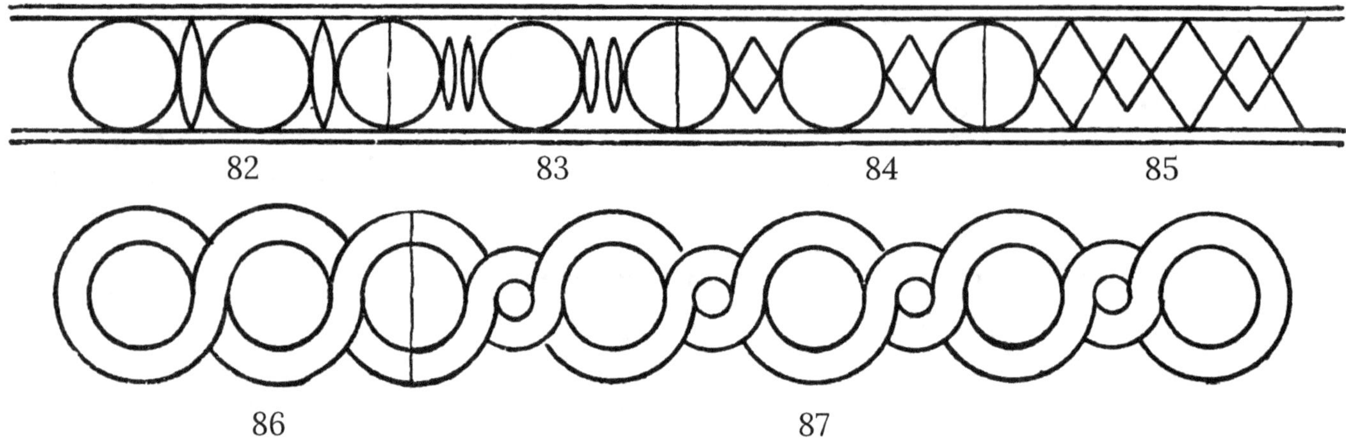

FIGURE 75. – Draw a vase with an elliptical bowl 1' wide, with a rectangular neck 1" wide, and 6" long.

FIGURE 76. – (1) Draw a vase with a rectangular-shaped bowl 8" wide and 6" high.

(2) Round the corners of the bowl.

(3) Draw the neck of the vase 2" wide and 5" long.

(4) Add to the top of the neck a keystone-shaped top.

FIGURE 77. – (1) Draw a goblet with an inverted keystone bowl.

(2) A plain rectangular stem.

(3) And a keystone-shaped standard.

FIGURE 78. – (1) Draw a vase with a rectangular-shaped bowl 9" wide and 5" high.

(2) Round the corners of the bowl.

(3) Add to this bowl a square stem 2" each way.

(4) Resting on a bell-shaped standard 6" wide.

(5) Add a rectangular-shaped neck 2" wide and 4" high, surmounted with a half lens-shaped top.

FIGURE 79. – Draw a border composed of a circle 5" in diameter alternating with a circle 3" in diameter.

FIGURE 80. – Draw a border composed of a circle 5" in diameter alternating with two circles 2" in diameter.

FIGURE 81. – Draw a border composed of a circle 5" in diameter alternating with two circles 2½" in diameter, placed one above the other.

FIGURE 82. – Draw a border composed of a circle 5" in diameter alternating with a vertical lens 5" long.

FIGURE 83. – Draw a border composed of a circle 5" in diameter alternating with two vertical lenses 3" long.

FIGURE 84. – Draw a border consisting of a circle 5" in diameter alternating with a diamond 2" wide and 3" high.

FIGURE 85. – Draw a border composed of a diamond 3" wide and 4" high, alternating with a diamond 2" wide and 3" high.

Each of these examples may be multiplied indefinitely.

FORM SUBSTITUTION.

Form substitution is simply substituting one form for another in the same manner that the different kinds of straight and curved lines were substituted for each other in line substitution.

The fruit dish, Fig. 88, is composed of rectangles and is the type for all of the fruit dishes, Figs. 88 - 93.

For the rectangular bowl in Fig. 88 is substituted a triangular bowl in Fig. 89, a semi-circular bowl in Fig. 90, a crescent-shaped bowl in Fig. 91, a conoid bowl in Fig. 92, and a keystone bowl in Fig. 93. In the same manner, the rectangular standard in Fig. 88 becomes triangular in Fig. 89, half lens-shaped in Fig. 90, bell-shaped in Fig. 91, conoid in Fig. 92, and keystone in Fig. 93. The rectangular ornament in the stem of Fig. 88 is changed in the same manner.

Form substitution may be combined with line substitution as in vases 94 - 101.

Vase 94 is the type. For the bell-shaped bowl of vase 94 is substituted the arrow-shaped bowl of vase 95, the heart-shaped bowl of vase 96, the kidney-shaped bowl of vase 97, the acorns in vases 98 and 99, the lens in vase 100, and the shield in vase 101. For the vertical lines of the neck in vase 94 are substituted inward curves in vase 95, outward curves in vase 96, etc.

The method may be taught as follows:

(1) Draw a simple object on the blackboard similar to Fig. 88, composed as much as possible of vertical and horizontal lines.

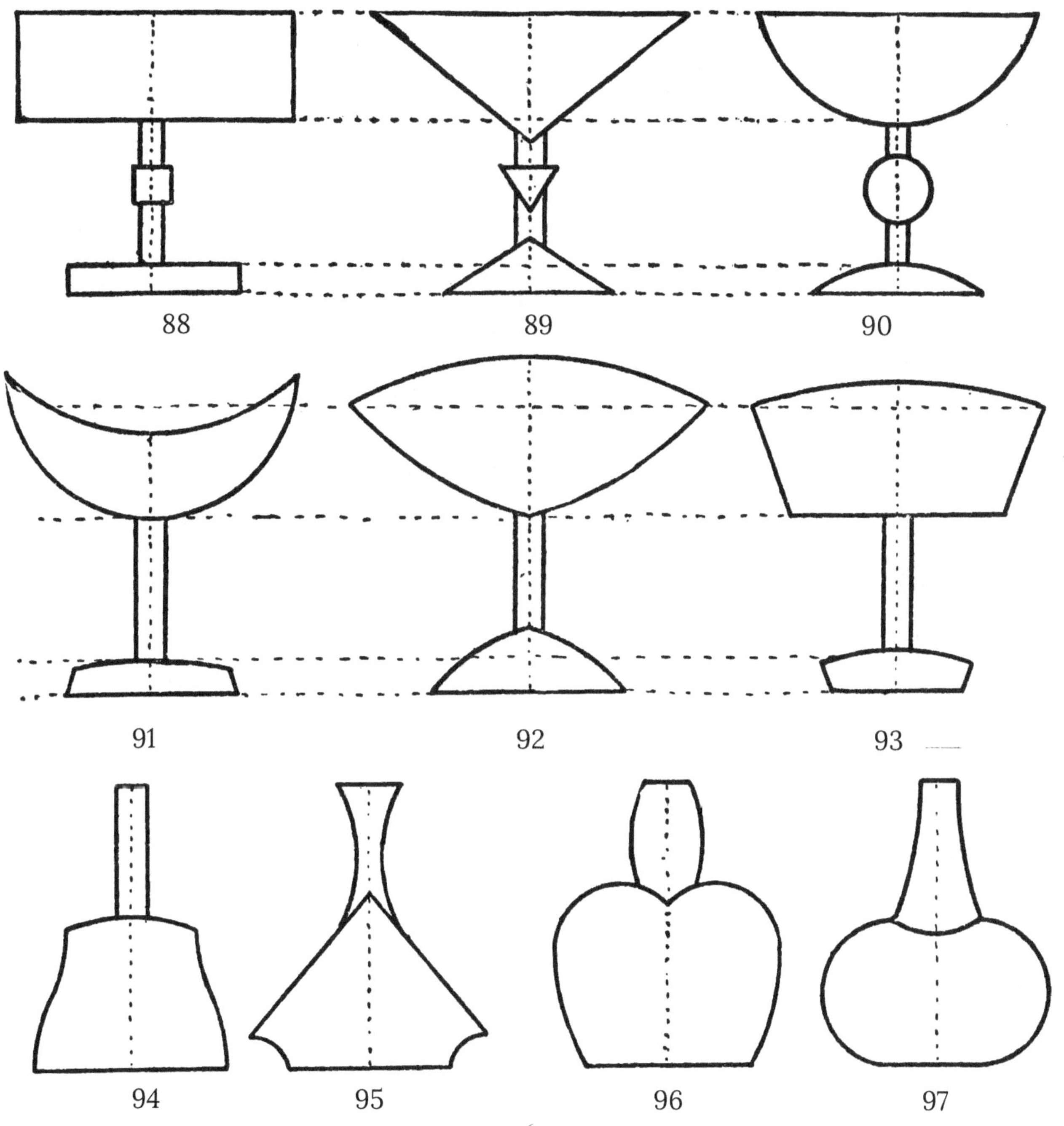

88
89
90
91
92
93
94
95
96
97

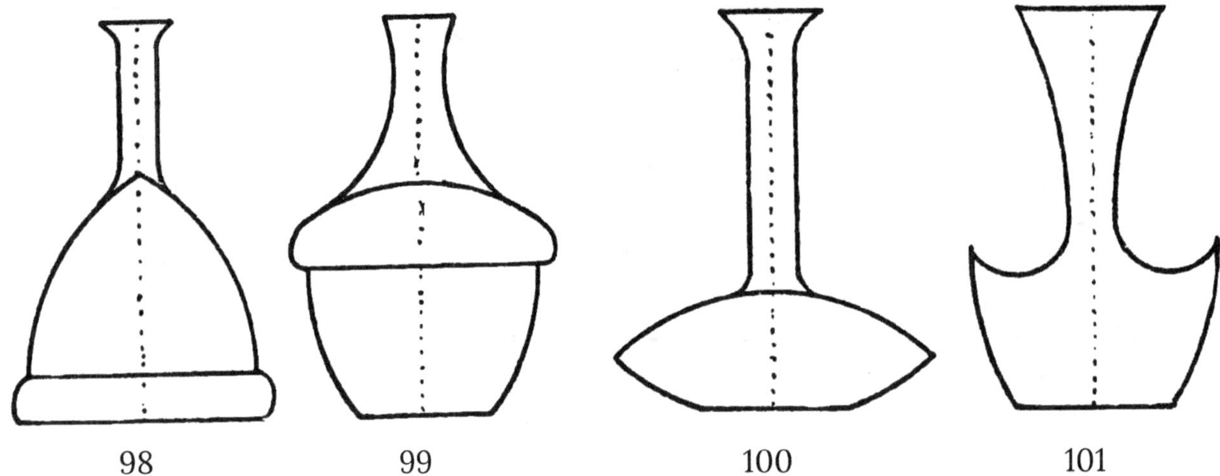

98   99   100   101

(2) Draw the figures you wish substituted on the blackboard, or

(3) Let the class draw similar objects by substituting Figs. 44 - 63 in the place of the different parts of the figure on the blackboard.

Any number of different figures may be substituted in the same object. For example, in Fig. 88 there may be substituted a crescent-shaped bowl, a lens-shaped stem, a bell-shaped standard, and a diamond ornament.

DESIGNING BY FORM.

Three steps are necessary when designing by form: (1) To know the object to be designed. (2) To place the parts, called units, of which the design is composed, where they can be seen. (3) To arrange these units forming the design.

Some knowledge of the object to be designed is necessary in order that similar ones may be made.

If a border is to be designed, simple borders should be shown to the class, the units pointed out, and how often they are repeated. It is well to separate the units of which the border is composed by drawing them separately on the blackboard and then uniting them again that the class may see how the border is formed.

To avoid confusion, not more than one unit should be used at first, and never more than two in a primary class.

For example, let us choose a border for the object to be designed and the unit of which it is composed — a square.

The squares may be arranged side by side as in Fig. 102, diamond-shaped as in Fig. 103, the diamond squares touching each other as in Fig. 104, the squares and the diamond squares alternating as in Fig. 105, the squares alternating with two diamond squares as in Fig. 106. The squares may be arranged in two rows, as in Fig. 117, or in three rows as in Fig. 118.

A large square may be made to alternate with a small square as in Fig. 107 and 108, or with two

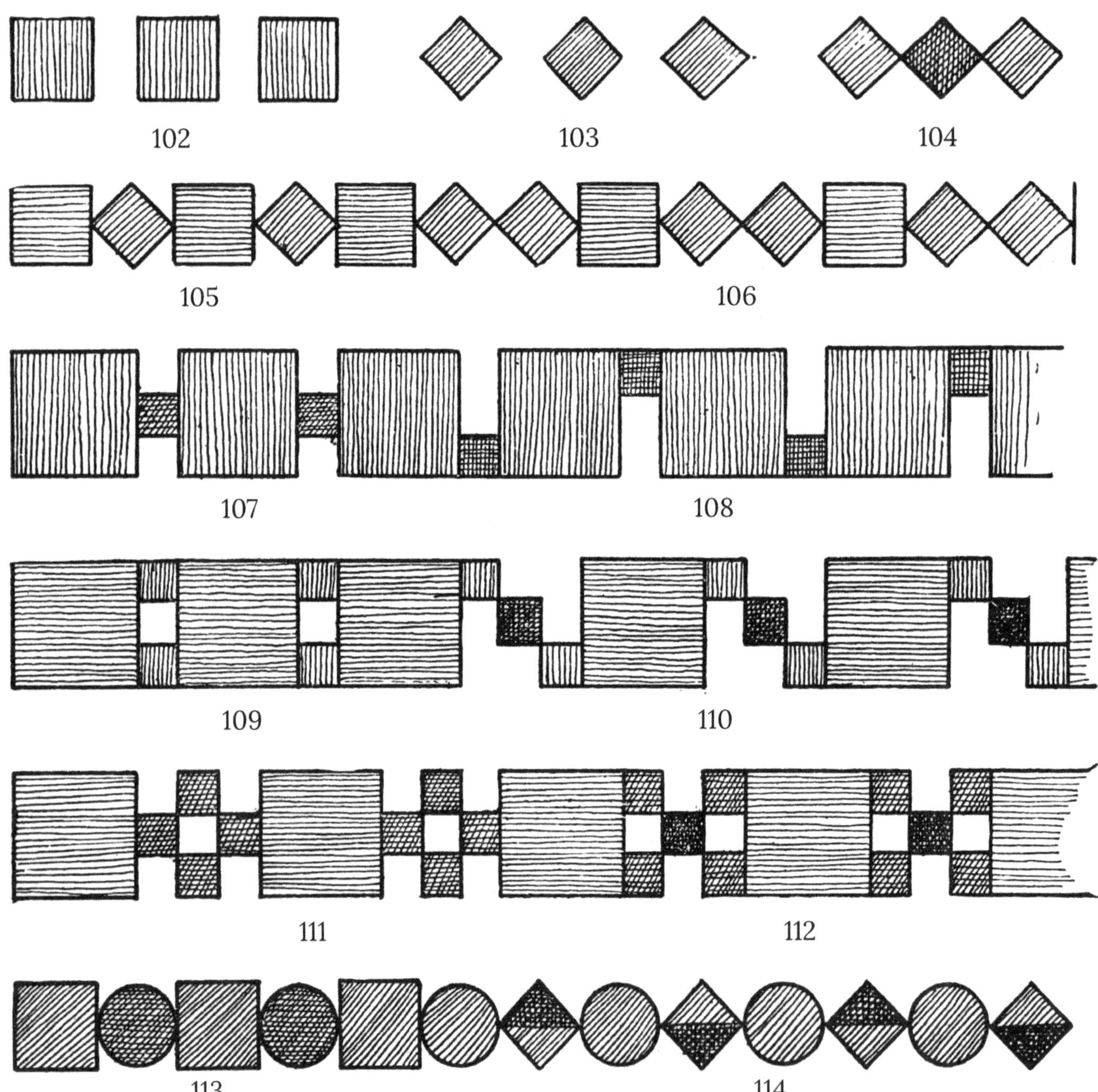

102   103   104

105   106

107   108

109   110

111   112

113   114

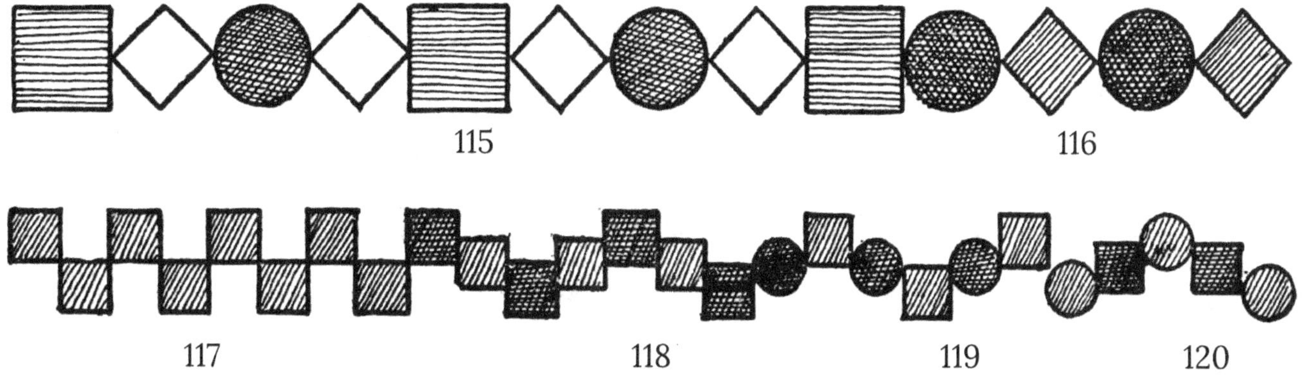

115   116

117   118   119   120

small squares as in Fig. 109, or with three small squares as in Fig. 110. A large square may be made to alternate with an ornament composed of squares as in Figs. 111 and 112.

Two figures or units may be arranged in a border, such as a square and circle. They may be made to alternate as in Figs. 113 and 114, or the square, diamond square, and circle as in Figs. 115 and 116. The two units may be made to alternate in three rows as in Figs. 119 and 120.

Figures 79, 80, and 81 are combinations of circles. Figs. 82 and 83 are combinations of circles and lenses. Fig. 84 shows circles and diamonds, Fig. 85 shows diamonds, and Figs. 86 and 87 show circles.

It will be seen that the number of combinations of even one unit in a common border is practically unlimited, and that by changing the relation of the units a new border is formed each time. By tinting the units with colors or shading them with crayon or lead pencil, still greater variety is obtained, and a new element, that of shading, is introduced into the drawing lesson.

If the pencil or crayon is used, the shading may be applied with straight lines as in the illustrations or by placing an even shade on the paper or board showing no lines.

One shade may be used as in Figs. 102, 103, 105, and 106, or two shades, as in Figs. 104, 107, 111, 118, etc., or three shades as in Figs. 112 and 115.

By means of form substitution, any form may be substituted in place of the squares. The triangle, rectangle, or any of the figures represented by Figs. 44–63 may be substituted in place of the squares. Different kinds of leaves may also be substituted, forming new borders.

The method may be taught as follows:

(1) Name the object to be designed, explaining its use, how it is made, and showing similar designs to the class. (2) Draw on the blackboard the units of which it is composed. (3) Unite these units in a simple design. (4) Let the pupils unite the same units in similar designs.

FIGURE 136 – 141 are ornaments made up of triangles.

FIGURE 141 is a star made up of units like the kite in Fig. 59. There is no limit to the number of combinations that can be made with these figures, and by combining two or more units, and by means of shading, the number is greatly increased and varied.

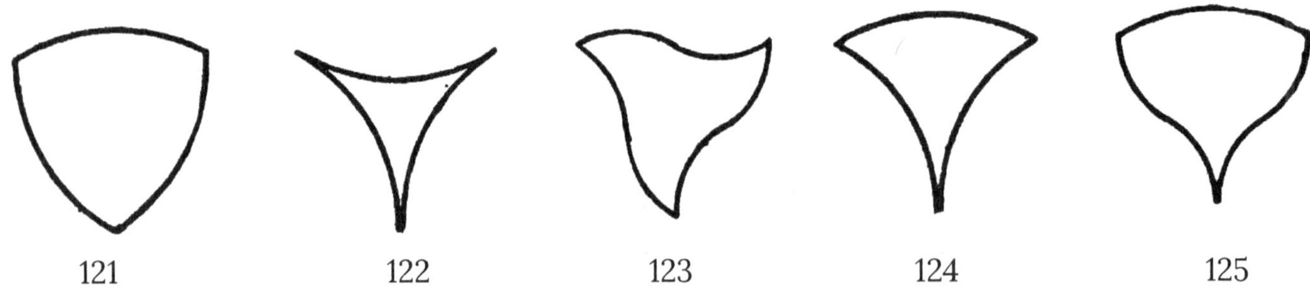

| 121 | 122 | 123 | 124 | 125 |

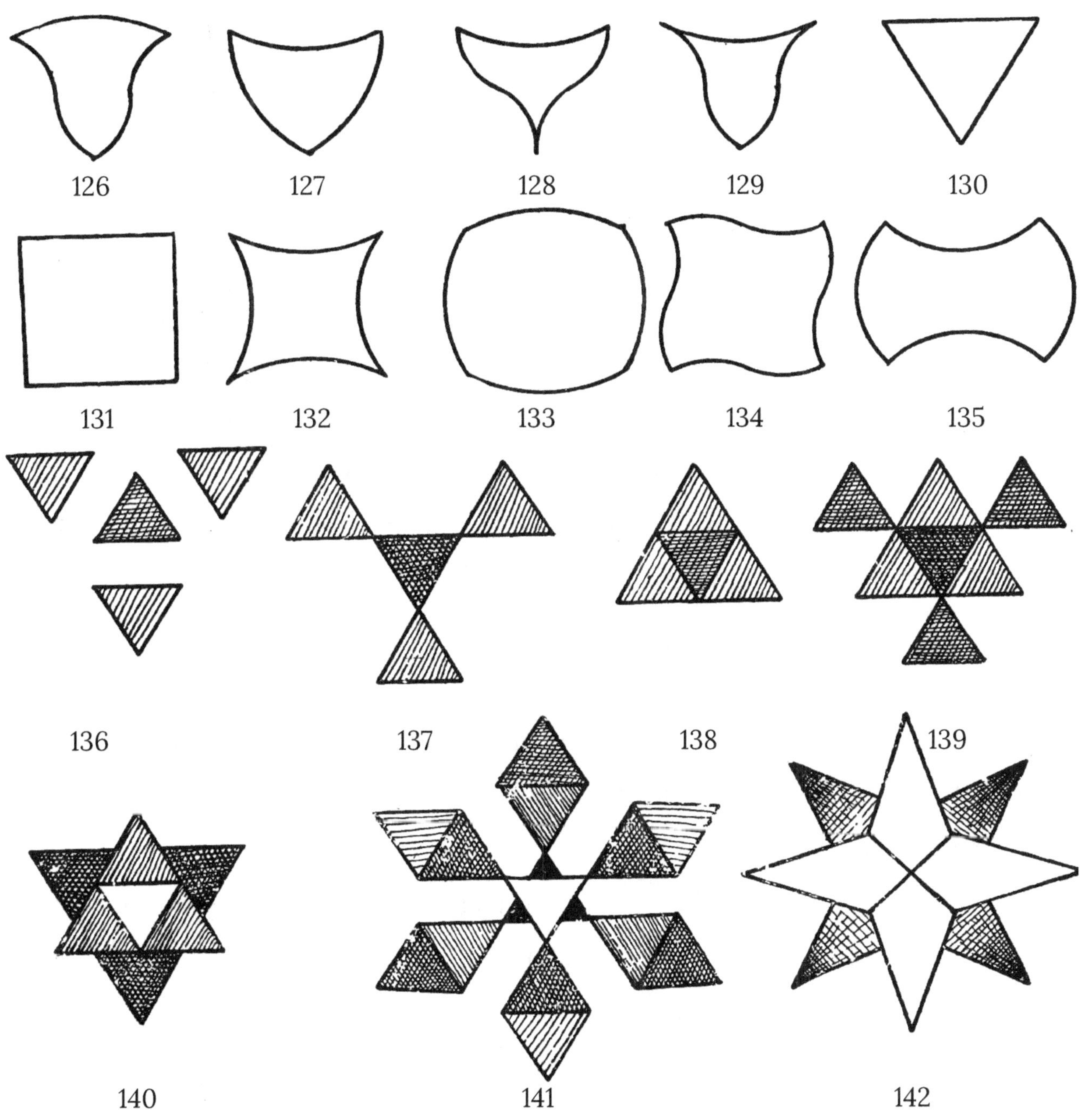

126 127 128 129 130

131 132 133 134 135

136 137 138 139

140 141 142

EASY PROBLEMS IN INVENTION.

(1) Draw an equilateral triangle (Fig. 130). (2) Substitute in place of the straight lines of the triangle outward curved lines (Fig. 121). (3) Inward curved lines (Fig. 122). (4) Double curved lines (Fig. 123). (5) One outward and two inward curved lines (Fig. 124). (6) One outward and two double curved lines (Fig. 125). (7) One outward and two inward curved lines (Fig. 126). (8) One inward and two outward curved lines (Fig. 127). (9) One inward and two double curved lines (Fig. 129).

(10) Draw a square (Fig. 131). (11) Substitute for the straight lines of the square inward curved lines (Fig. 132). (12) Outward curved lines (Fig. 133). (13) Double curved lines (Fig. 134). (14) Substitute in place of the horizontal lines inward curves, and in place of the vertical lines, outward curved lines.

(15) Draw a kite form (Fig. 59). (16) Substitute in place of the straight lines inward curves. (17) Outward curves. (18) Double curves. (19) In place of the upper lines, outward curves, and in place of the lower lines, inward curves, etc.

(20) Dictate by line (Fig. 10).

(21) Dictate by line (Fig. 22). (22) Dictate by line (Fig. 24). (23) Dictate by line (Fig. 37).

(24) Substitute for the vertical lines of the bowl in Fig. 88 oblique outward curves. For the upper part of the stem inward curves. For the lower part of the stem outward curves. Substitute in place of the straight lines of the ornament in the stem outward curves.

(25) Substitute for the straight lines of Fig. 89 outward and inward curves.

(26) Draw by substitution four wine glasses similar to Fig. 73.

(27) Draw by line substitution four vases similar to Fig. 78.

(28) Substitute in Fig. 73 a fan-shaped bowl and an inverted funnel for the standard.

(29) Substitute in place of the squares in Fig. 102, acorns, shields, and fans.

(30) Substitute in place of the diamond squares of Fig. 104, Fig. 124.

(31) Substitute an ellipse in place of the squares in Fig. 105.

(32) Make Fig. 61 alternate with Fig. 58 in a border.

(33) Make Fig. 60 alternate with Fig. 58 in a border.

(34) Make Fig. 129 alternate with a small circle.

(35) Substitute triangles in place of the lower row of Fig. 117.

(36) Substitute Fig. 55 in place of the squares in Fig. 113, and lenses in place of the circles.

(37) Substitute Fig. 63 in place of the diamond squares of Fig. 104.

(38) Arrange Fig. 49 and a small circle into a border.

(39) Make Fig. 137 alternate with a large square as in Fig. 111.

www.ingramcontent.com/pod-product-compliance
Lightning Source LLC
Chambersburg PA
CBHW082122180726
48291CB00011B/2813